TIGRELA
AND OTHER
STORIES

by Lygia Fagundes Telles

Translated by
Margaret A. Neves

A BARD BOOK/PUBLISHED BY AVON BOOKS

Originally published as *Seminario dos Ratos* by Livraria Jose Olympio Editora.

TIGRELA AND OTHER STORIES is an original publication of Avon Books. This work has never before appeared in book form. This is a work of fiction. Any similarity to actual persons or events is purely coincidental.

AVON BOOKS
A division of
The Hearst Corporation
1790 Broadway
New York, New York 10019

Copyright © 1977 by Lygia Fagundes Telles
Translation copyright © 1986 by Margaret A. Neves
Published by arrangement with the author
Library of Congress Catalog Card Number: 85-91192
ISBN: 0-380-89627-3

First Bard Printing, May 1986

BARD TRADEMARK REG. U.S. PAT. OFF. AND IN
OTHER COUNTRIES, MARCA REGISTRADA, HECHO EN
U.S.A.

Printed in the U.S.A.

OPM 10 9 8 7 6 5 4 3 2 1

LYGIA FAGUNDES TELLES was born in São Paulo, Brazil, but spent her childhood in small towns in the state where her father served as district attorney, police commissioner, and a judge. This childhood experience provided the imaginative background for many of her stories. Today she is a lawyer and president of the Brazilian Cinematheque, founded by her late husband, film critic and author Paulo Emilio Salles Gomes, whose novel *P.'s Three Women* is available from Avon Books.

Lygia Fagundes Telles has published three novels, a half dozen novellas, and seven short story collections. In 1969 she was awarded the Cannes Prix International des Femmes for her short story "Before the Green Masquerade," chosen from among the works of authors from twenty-one countries. In addition to TIGRELA, Avon publishes two other works by Ms. Telles—her first novel, THE MARBLE DANCE, and the award-winning THE GIRL IN THE PHOTOGRAPH.

Other Avon Bard Books by
Lygia Fagundes Telles

THE GIRL IN THE PHOTOGRAPH
THE MARBLE DANCE

Contents

The Ants

When my cousin and I got out of the taxi, it was almost dark. We stood motionless before the old two-story house with oval windows, just like two melancholy eyes, one of them broken by a hurled rock. I rested my suitcase on the ground and took my cousin by the arm.

"It's sinister."

She pulled me toward the door. Did we have any other choice? For two penniless students, no other boarding-house in the area offered a better price, with permission to use the single-burner stove in the room, the landlady had advised us over the phone that we could cook light meals on the condition we didn't start a fire. We went up the ancient staircase, which smelled of creosote.

"At least I don't see any sign of cockroaches," said my cousin.

The landlady was a swollen old crone, with a wig blacker than a crow's wing. She wore a faded pair of Japanese silk pajamas, and her crooked fingernails were covered with a crust of dark-red enamel, faded and peeling off at the edges. She lighted up a cheroot.

"Are you the one who studies medicine?" she asked, blowing smoke in my direction.

"I study law. She's medicine."

The woman looked at us indifferently. She must have been thinking about something else as she blew out a cloud of smoke so dense I had to turn aside. The little parlor was dark, crammed with old, unmatched furniture. On the holy straw seat of the sofa were two pillows, which apparently had been made from the remains of an old dress, the embroidery interspersed with sequins.

"I'll show you the room, it's in the attic," she said in the middle of an attack of coughing and motioned us to follow her.

"The last tenant studied medicine, too. He left behind a little box of bones, which he was supposed to come after. But up to now he hasn't appeared."

My cousin stopped. "A box of bones?"

The woman didn't answer, concentrated on the effort of going up the narrow winding staircase, which led to the room. She turned on the light. The room couldn't have been any smaller, with the ceiling sloping downward so sharply that in one part we would have to crawl. Two beds, two wardrobes, a table, and a straw-backed chair painted gold. In the angle where the ceiling almost met the floor, there was a small crate covered with a sheet of plastic. My cousin set down her suitcase and, kneeling, pulled out the crate by its rope handle. She lifted up the plastic, seemingly fascinated.

"But what tiny little bones! Are they a child's?"

"He said they were an adult's. A dwarf's."

"A dwarf's? You're right, you can see that they're already formed. But what a find, dwarf skeletons are rare as anything. And so clean, look here," she marveled. With her fingertips she brought out a tiny skull of a limelike whiteness.

"So perfect! Every single tooth!"

"I was going to throw the whole thing in the trash, but if you're interested, you can keep it. The bathroom is here at the side, you're the only ones who will use it, mine is downstairs. Hot baths extra. Phone also. Supper's from seven to nine, I'll leave the table set in the kitchen with coffee in the thermos, close it tight," she recommended, scratching her head. The wig slipped slightly out of kilter. She blew out a final cloud of smoke. 'Don't leave the door open or my cat will get out."

We stood there looking at each other and laughing while

we listened to the sound of her high-heeled slippers on the stairs. And her catarrhal cough.

I emptied my suitcase, hung up my wrinkled blouse on a hanger, which I stuck into a crack in the venetian blind, taped a Grassmann engraving on the wall, and set my plush teddy bear on the pillow. I watched my cousin climb up on a chair, unscrew the very weak light bulb that was hanging from a solitary wire in the middle of the ceiling, and replace it with a 200-watt bulb she took from her bag. The room became more cheerful. On the other hand, we could now see that the bed linen was not so white, white was the small tibia she took from the crate and examined. She picked up a vertebra and looked through the opening as small as the circumference of a ring. Delicately she put them away, as if she were arranging eggs in a basket.

"A dwarf? Very rare, understand? And I don't think any of the bones are missing, I'm going to bring the ligatures, maybe I can start putting him together this weekend."

We opened a can of sardines, which we ate with bread, my cousin always had a can of something stashed away, she often studied into the wee hours and afterward made herself a snack. When the bread was gone, she opened a package of biscuits.

"Where is that smell coming from?" I asked, sniffing. I went over to the crate, came back, smelled the floor. "Don't you notice a sour smell?"

"It's mildew. The whole house smells that way," she said. And she pushed the crate under the bed.

In the dream a blond dwarf wearing a plaid vest and hair parted down the middle came into the room. He was smoking a cigar. He sat down on my cousin's bed, crossed his short legs, and sat there with a very serious expression, watching her sleep. I wanted to scream, "There's a dwarf in the room!" but before I could manage to, I woke up. The light was on. On hands and knees, still dressed, my cousin was staring at something on the floor.

"What are you doing there?" I asked.

"These ants. All of a sudden they just appeared, grouped together. So purposeful, do you see them?" I got up, and was met with the small red ants, which were entering in a solid line through the crack under the door, crossing the room, marching up the side of the small box of bones, and swarming inside, disciplined as an army on parade.

"There are thousands, I've never seen so many ants. And there's no return line, only a line coming," I puzzled.

"Only coming."

I told her about my nightmare with the dwarf seated on her bed.

"He's underneath it," said my cousin. And she pulled the box out. She took off the plastic. "It's black with ants. Give me the bottle of alcohol."

"There must be something left there on these bones, and they've discovered it, ants discover everything. If I were you, I'd take this outside."

"But the bones are completely clean, I tell you. There's not even a thread of cartilege left. Superclean. I wonder what these bandits came looking for in here."

She sprinkled alcohol liberally all over the crate. Then, she put on her shoes and like a tightrope walker balancing on a high wire, she stepped firmly, one foot in front of the other, on the line of ants. She went back and forth twice. Putting out her cigarette, she pulled up the chair and sat looking into the box.

"Odd. Very odd."

"What?"

"I remember putting the cranium right on top of the pile, I even put the shoulder blades under it so it wouldn't roll. And now it's there on the bottom of the case with a shoulder blade on each side. Did you by any chance mess around in here?"

"God forbid, bones give me the creeps. Especially dwarf bones."

She covered the small crate with the sheet of plastic, pushed it away with her foot, and put the hot plate on the table, it was time for her tea. On the floor, the line of dead ants was now a dark shrunken ribbon. One ant which had escaped the slaughter passed by near my foot, I was just going to squash it when I saw it bring its hands up to its head, like a despairing person. I let it disappear into a crack in the floor.

My sleep was riddled by nightmares again, but this time it was the old dream about exams, the professor asking question after question and I silent, confronted by the one point I hadn't studied. At six A.M. the alarm clock rang vehemently. I turned the bell off. My cousin was asleep with her head covered. In the bathroom I peered closely at the walls, the cement floor, looking for them. I didn't see any. I went back on tiptoe and opened the venetian blinds slightly. The suspicious smell of the night before disappeared. I looked at the floor: the ranks of the massacred army had vanished too. I glanced under the bed and didn't see the slightest movement of ants on the covered case.

When I got back around seven that night, my cousin was already in the room. I found her looking so worn-out that I put extra salt in her omelette; she had low blood pressure. We ate in a voracious silence. Then I remembered.

"And the ants?"

"None, up to now."

"Did you sweep up the dead ones?"

She stared at me. "I didn't sweep up anything, I was exhausted. Wasn't it you?"

"Me! When I woke up, there wasn't any sign of ants on this floor, I was sure that before going to bed you had cleaned them up. But then who—?"

Squinting, she blinked her eyes, she went cross-eyed when she was worried.

"Really very weird. Superweird."

I went to get a chocolate bar and near the door I again noticed the odor, but could it be mildew? It didn't seem like such an innocent smell to me, I wanted to call my cousin's attention to it but she seemed so depressed I decided it was better to keep quiet.

I sprinkled apple-blossom cologne all over the room (so what if it smelled like an orchard) and went to bed early. I had the second type of bad dream, which competed with the exam nightmare for repetition; in this one, I made a date to meet two different boyfriends in the same place, at the same time. The first one would come and I would go crazy trying to get him away from there before the second one showed up. In this dream the second one was the dwarf. When nothing remained but hollowed-out shadow and silence, my cousin's voice snagged me with its hook. I opened my eyes with an effort. She was sitting on the edge of my bed, wearing her pajamas, completely cross-eyed.

"They're back."

"Who?"

"The ants. They only attack at night, in the wee hours. They're all here again."

Last night's army, compact and intense, followed its former course from the door to the box of bones, up which it climbed in the same formation until disbanding inside. Without a return file.

"And the bones?"

She rolled herself up in the blanket, she was trembling.

"That's just it. Something's happening, I don't understand it at all. I got up to do pee-pee, it must have been about three o'clock. On my way back to bed I felt that there was *something else* in the room, you know? I looked at the floor and saw the solid line of ants, you remember? There wasn't one when we got here. I went to look at the box; they were all milling around inside, of course, but that wasn't what almost made me fall over backward, there's something more serious: The bones are actually changing position. I already suspected it, but now I'm sure, little by little they're . . . they're being organized."

"Organized, how?"

She became thoughtful. I began to shake with cold, and grabbed a corner of her blanket. I covered my teddy bear up with the sheet.

"You remember, the cranium between the shoulder blades, I didn't put it there. Now the spinal column is almost formed, one vertebra after the other, each little bone in its place, somebody who knows his business is putting the skeleton together, a little bit more and—come see!"

"I believe you, I don't want to see anything. They're putting the dwarf back together, is that it?"

We watched the rapid line, the ants marching so close

together that not even a particle of dust would fit between them. I hopped over it with the greatest of care as I went to heat up some tea. One ant which was out of line (the same one as the other night?) was shaking its head between its hands. I began to laugh so hard that if the floor hadn't been occupied, I would have rolled on it. We fell asleep together in my bed. She was still asleep when I went out for my first class. On the floor, not the shadow of an ant, dead or alive, they disappeared with the light of day.

I went back late that night, a classmate had gotten married, and there was a party. I came home happy, in the mood to sing, I'd had a few too many. Then as I was going upstairs I remembered: the dwarf. My cousin had dragged the table over to the door, and was studying with the kettle bubbling on the hot plate.

"Tonight I'm not going to sleep, I want to keep watch," she announced. The floor was still clean. I hugged the bear to me.

"I'm scared."

She went to get me an aspirin to lessen my hangover, made me swallow it with a gulp of tea, and helped me get undressed.

"I'll stay up watching, you can sleep in peace. So far they haven't appeared, it's not time for them yet, they usually start later. I examined under the door with a magnifying glass, you know I couldn't discover where they come from?"

I flopped onto the bed, I don't think I even answered. At the head of the stairs the dwarf grabbed my wrists and whirled me into the bedroom: wake up, wake up! It took me a moment to recognize my cousin, who was holding me by the elbows. She was livid. And squinting.

"They came back," she said.

I held my throbbing head between my hands.

"Are they there?"

She spoke in a small voice, as if it were a little ant speaking.

"I ended up falling asleep over the table, I was exhausted. When I woke up, the line was already there in full march.

So I went and looked in the box, and it happened just as I expected . . ."

"What, tell me quick, what?"

She fixed her oblique glance on the small crate under the bed.

"They really are putting him together, and fast, understand? The skeleton is almost complete, they only need to put the femur in place. And the little bones of the left hand, they'll do that in no time. Let's get out of here."

"Are you serious?"

"Let's go, I've already packed the bags." The table was bare and the wide-open closet empty.

"But to go off like this, in the middle of the night? Can we just leave this way?"

"Immediately, better not wait for the witch to wake up. Come on, get up."

"And where will we go?"

"It doesn't matter, later we'll see. Hurry up, put this on, we have to get out before they get the dwarf ready."

I looked at the line from a distance; they had never seemed to move so fast. I put on my shoes, unstuck my engraving from the wall, jammed the bear into the pocket of my jacket, and we went lugging the suitcases down the steps, the smell from the room coming stronger now, we had left the door open. Was it the cat that gave a long meow or a cry?

In the sky, the last stars were fading. When I turned to look back at the house, only the broken window watched us, the other eye was in shadow.

Rat Seminar

"Que século, meu Deus!—exclamaram os ratos e começaram a roer o edifício."
—Carlos Drummond de Andrade

The Chief of Public Relations, a short, stout man with extremely bright smile and eyes, straightened the knot in his red tie and knocked lightly at the door of the Secretary of Public and Private Welfare.

"Excellency?"

The Secretary of Public and Private Welfare set the glass of milk on the table and swiveled his leather armchair round. He sighed. He was a colorless, flaccid man with a damp bald head and stainy hands. He gazed lengthily at his feet, the right one shod, the left one stuck into a thick woolen slipper with leather edging.

"Come in," he said to the Chief of Public Relations, who was already peeping through the crack in the door. He folded his hands together over his chest. "So? Did the cocktail party go all right?"

His voice was mild, with a slightly mournful lilt. The young man drew himself up. A faint blush covered his close-shaven face.

"Everything perfect, Excellency. Perfect. It was in the Blue Salon, which as your Excellency knows is smaller. Very few people, just the leadership, which made it a cozy meeting, intimate but very pleasant. I performed the

9

introductions"—he simpered—"and"—he consulted his watch—"barely six o'clock, and they've already broken up. The Adviser to the Presidency of RATESP is installed in the North Wing, across from the Director of the Armed and Unarmed Conservative Classes, who is occupying the Gray Suite. Now, I thought it convenient to install the American Delegation in the South Wing. By the way, I left them just a little while ago in the swimming pool, the sunset is dazzling, Excellency, dazzling!"

"You said the Director of the Armed and Unarmed Conservative Classes is staying in the Gray Suite. Why *gray*?"

The young man asked permission to sit down. He pulled up his chair but maintained a prudent distance from the pillow where the Secretary rested his slippered foot. He cleared his throat.

"*Bueno*, I chose the colors with the persons in mind," he began with a certain hesitation. Brightening—"the American Delegation's suite, for example, is bright pink, they like lively colors. For your Excellency, I chose this pastel blue; more than once I've seen your Excellency with a blue tie . . . and so, gray occurred to me for the North Suite, doesn't your Excellency like gray? It seems so tranquilizing to me . . ."

With difficulty the Secretary moved the foot extended on the pillow. He raised his hand and stared at it.

"It's *their* color. *Rattus Alexandrius*."

"Of the Conservatives?"

"No, of the rats. But never mind, it isn't important; go ahead, please. You were saying that the Americans are in the swimming pool, why American*s*, plural? Did more than one come?"

"Well, a secretary came with the Massachusetts Delegate, a lovely girl! And a red-haired fellow with a plaid suit, sort of a boxer type, rather quiet, always beside the other two. I think he's a bodyguard, but that's mere supposition, Excellency; the gentleman in question is a mystery. They speak only English. I took advantage of the opportunity to talk with them, I finished my executives' English course a short time ago, if the debates are in English as proposed, I'll give my full collaboration. However modest. Now Spanish I dominate perfectly, I lived in Buenos Aires for two years . . ."

"I was against his suggestion. This American's," the Secretary interrupted in a soft but pained tone. "The rats are ours, the solutions have to be ours. Why demonstrate our flaws to everybody else? Our deficiencies? We should show only the positive side, not only of the society but of our own household. Of ourselves," he added, pointing to his foot on the pillow.

"Why haven't I appeared yet? Simply because I don't want them to see me indisposed, with a swollen foot, limping. Tomorrow I'll put on a shoe for the installation, I make that sacrifice willingly. You, who are a potential candidate, should learn these things early off, young man. Show only the positive side, only that which can build us up. Hide our slippers."

"But, Excellency, this American is a technician in rats, there are a lot of them in the United States, too; he'll be able to give us valuable suggestions. What's more, I found out that he's an expert in electronic journalism."

"Worse yet. He'll go tooting his horn all over," sighed the Secretary as he tried to change the position of his foot. "But never mind, it's not important. Go ahead, please. I want you to inform me about the repercussion. Among the press, of course."

The Chief of Public Relations cleared his throat discreetly, murmured a "*bueno*" and patted his pockets. He asked permission to smoke.

"*Bueno*, your Excellency is aware that our choice of this locale has caused astonishment: Why install the Seventh Seminar of Rodents in a completely isolated country house? That's the first general criticism. The second is that we spent too much money to make this mansion habitable, a waste when we had other places ready at our disposal. Some reporter from an afternoon paper, I took care to remember his face, Excellency, this so-and-so was actually insolent when he snarled that there were so many buildings available, that the implosions are already multiplying to correct the excess. While we spend millions to restore this ruin . . .''

The Secretary wiped his bald head and tried to settle himself more comfortably. He began a gesture which he didn't finish.

"We, spending millions? These demons are consuming billions, does he by chance ignore the statistics? I'm betting he's a leftist, I'm betting on it. Or else a friend of the rats. But never mind, it's not important. Go ahead, please.''

"These are the severest criticisms, Excellency. Smalltime stuff. Oh, and the eternal tune they keep playing, that the rat population has multiplied itself seven times since the first Seminar, that we now have seven rats for each inhabitant, that in the slums it's not the Marias but the she-rats who carry cans of water on their heads,'' he added, stifling a little laugh. "Small-time stuff. What they can't accept is our meeting in a remote place, they say we should be in the central areas, in the midst of the problem. Our Press Adviser has again clarified the crystal-clear truth, that this Seminar is the headquarters of a real battle! Imagine, to outline a joint action of this import demands meditation, lucidity! Where else could you gentlemen work if not here, breathing the air that only the country can offer? In this blessed solitude, in intimate contact with nature! . . . the Massachusetts Delegate found the idea of meeting in the middle of the country very agreeable. As a matter of fact, he's a wonderful fellow, so unsophisticated. He thought our thermal swimming pool was excellent, did your Excellency know? he was a champion breaststroke swimmer, he's down there enjoying himself, he adored drinking our coconut water! He told me the funniest thing, that the rats of the North Pole have enormous skins to withstand the thirty-below-zero cold, the scoundrels have fitted themselves out with furs! They could live on Mars, constitutions of iron . . . !''

The Secretary appeared to be thinking about something else, when he murmured an evasive "never mind.'' He raised his finger, requesting silence, and looked suspiciously at the rug, then at the ceiling.

"What's that noise?''

"Noise?"

"A strange noise, don't you hear it?"

The Chief of Public Relations cocked his head, concentrating.

"I don't hear anything . . ."

"It's getting fainter," said the Secretary, lowering his puffy finger. "Now it's stopped. But didn't you hear it? Such an odd noise, as if it were coming from below the ground, then it went up to the ceiling . . . are you sure you didn't hear it?"

The young man opened his innocent blue eyes wide.

"Absolutely nothing, Excellency. But was it here in the room?"

"Or outside, I don't know. As if somebody . . ." He took out his handkerchief, wiped his mouth, and let out a long breath. "It wouldn't come as a shock to me if they'd been presumptuous enough to put a bug in here. Do you remember? This American Delegate . . ."

"But, Excellency, he's the guest of the Director of the Armed and Unarmed Classes!"

"I don't trust anyone. Or almost anyone," the Secretary corrected in a whisper. He cast a suspicious glance at the table, at the blue canopy over the bed. "Wherever these people are, there's always a cursed tape recorder. Never mind, it doesn't matter, go ahead, please. And the Press Adviser?"

"*Bueno*, last night he suffered a slight accident, your Excellency knows how our traffic is! He had to have his arm put in a cast, he can't get here until tomorrow, I've already arranged for a little jet," added the young man energetically. "There will be an armed team in the rearguard for cover. Our Adviser will leak the news by telephone, creating suspense until the close of the Seminar, when they will all come in special planes, photographers, television networks, foreign correspondents, an apotheosis, *finis coronat opus*! The end crowns the work!"

"All I know is, he should be here, it's a bad way to start," lamented the Secretary as he bent toward the glass of milk. He took a swallow and said disapprovingly, "After all, what worries me most is for us to remain incommunicable. I really don't know if this idea of the Adviser to the Presidency of RATESP is going to work, of keeping the reporters out. I have my doubts.''

''Your Excellency will pardon me, but I think the leadership increases its prestige by staying inaccessible this way. In fact, it's well known that a certain distance, a certain mystery, excites the public more than daily contact with the media. Our only informant will let out discreet statements, influencing without alarm until the end, when we'll open the batteries! Isn't that good tactics?''

With drumming fingers, the Secretary vaguely stroked his vest buttons. He laced his hands together and gazed at his polished fingernails.

''Good tactics, my boy, is to influence all the country's means of communication from beginning to end. That's the objective. Which is already jeopardized with this Adviser breaking his leg.''

''Arm, Excellency. The forearm, more precisely.''

The Secretary shifted his body painfully to the right, then to the left. He mopped his forehead, the spaces between his fingers, and stared at his propped-up foot.

''You could call him yet today and say that, strategically speaking, the rats are under control. Without details, just emphasize that, that the rats are already completely under control. Does the connection take long?''

''*Bueno*, about half an hour. Shall I ask for it at once, Excellency?''

The Secretary was lifting his finger. He opened his mouth and swung the chair toward the window. With the same slow motions, he turned back in the direction of the fireplace.

''Do you hear it? Do you hear it? The noise, it's louder now!''

The young man cupped his hand behind his ear. His forehead flushed with the effort of concentration. He got up, moving on tiptoe.

''Is it coming from there, Excellency? I can't hear anything.''

''It gets louder and softer, there, in waves, like the sea . . . now it's like a volcano breathing, close by yet at the same time so far away! There, it's fading . . ." He flopped back onto the chair, exhausted, and dried his damp chin. "You mean you didn't hear anything at all?"

The Chief of Public Relations arched his perplexed eyebrows. He peered into the fireplace, behind the chair. Raising the window curtains, he looked out into the garden.

"There are two servants out on the lawn, chauffeurs, I suppose . . . Hey! You there!" he called, waving. He closed the window. "They disappeared. They seemed agitated, maybe they were arguing, but I don't imagine it had anything to do with the sound. And I'm unable to help, Excellency, I hear so badly with this ear! Sorry . . . !"

"Well, I hear all too well. I must have an extra eardrum. So sensitive. When I took part in the Revolution, in '32 and later in '64, I was always the first one in the group to sense any abnormality. The first! I remember one night I warned my companions, the enemy is here, and they laughed, nonsense, you drank too much wine! We had drunk a delicious wine at dinner. Well, when we were leaving to go to bed, we found ourselves surrounded."

The Chief of Public Relations looked distrustfully at the bronze statuette on the mantelpiece, an opulent blindfolded woman clutching the sword and the scales. Stretching his hand out toward the scales, he rubbed a finger over one of its dusty trays. He took a look at his finger and cleaned it furtively on the back of the armchair.

"Would your Excellency like me to go take a sounding?"

The Secretary extended his leg wincingly and sighed.

"Never mind, it's not important. During these crises of mine, I'm capable of hearing somebody strike a match in the living room."

Somewhere between consternated and timid, the young man gestured toward the lame foot.

"Is it anything . . . serious?"

"The gout."

"And does it hurt, Excellency?"

"A great deal."

"*It could be a drop of water! It could be a drop of*

water!'' he caroled, widening the smile which quickly drooped in the taciturn silence following his musical intervention. He cleared his throat and adjusted the knot in his tie. *"Bueno*, it's a song the people sing."

"The people, the people," said the Secretary of Public and Private Welfare, folding his hands. His voice became a mild grumble. "All you hear is 'the People,' and yet the people are nothing more than an abstraction."

"Abstraction, Excellency?"

"Which transforms itself into reality when the rats start to turn the slum dwellers out of their houses. Or chew the feet of the children on the periphery . . . then, yes, *the people* start to exist in the left-wing press headlines. The underground press, in other words, pure demagogy. Allied with the subversive bombs, we mustn't forget those bastards, they're just like the rats," sighed the Secretary, running his fingers over his vest buttons. He undid the last one.

"In ancient Egypt they solved this problem by increasing the number of cats. I don't know why they don't demand more private incentive here, if each family had one or two starving cats at home . . ."

"But, Excellency, there aren't any cats left in the city, it's been some time since the population ate them all. I've heard they make an excellent stew!"

"Never mind," murmured the Secretary, starting to make a motion and checking himself. "It's getting dark, isn't it?"

The young man got up to turn on the lights. His eyes smiled intensely: "And all cats are black at night!" Then, serious, "Almost seven o'clock, your Excellency. Dinner will be served at eight, the table decorated with nothing but fruit and orchids, the finest local color, truly splendid! I ordered the most beautiful pineapples from the north! And the lobsters! The Chief Cook was most enthusiastic, he had never seen such big ones. *Bueno*, I had thought, in

---

*Translator's note: The word for "drop" in Portuguese is "gota," which is also the word for "gout." The Chief of Public Relations was attempting to cheer his superior with a pun.

passing you might say, about a domestic wine which is presently first-rate, but a certain misgiving came over me, what if it caused somebody a headache? If on account of some such misfortune, can your Excellency imagine? So I thought it prudent to order Chilean wine.''

''What vintage?''

''Pinochet, naturally.''

The Secretary of Public and Private Welfare lowered his resentful gaze to his own foot.

''For me, some broth without salt, a thin chicken soup. Later perhaps an . . .'' he broke off. Gaping, he swung slowly around toward the young man.

''Do you hear it now? It's stronger, hear that? Very strong!''

The Chief of Public Relations jumped up, clutching his reddened face between his hands.

''But of course, Excellency, it's echoing here in the floor, the floor is quaking! But what is it?''

''Didn't I tell you? Didn't I tell you?'' cried the Secretary, seemingly triumphant. ''I've never been mistaken, never! I've been hearing things for hours, but I didn't want to say anything, they might think I was delirious, and now look! We're in what seems to be a volcanic zone, as if a volcano were going to erupt right under us!''

''Volcano?''

''Or a bomb, there are bombs that give out warnings before they explode!''

''My God!'' exclaimed the young man. He ran to the door. ''I'll find out about this immediately, Excellency, don't worry, it can't be anything, excuse me, I'll be right back. My God, a volcanic zone!''

As he slammed the door behind him, another opened opposite, and a blondly smiling face appeared in the opening. Her hair was caught on top of her head with a bow of yellow polka-dot ribbon.

''What's that?''

''Perhaps nothing, perhaps something,'' he answered, grinning his automatic grin. He waved to her with a flutter of fingers imitating wings. ''Supper at eight, Miss Gloria!''

He walked faster when he saw the Director of Armed

and Unarmed Conservative Classes, who was approaching in his green velvet bathrobe. He shrank back to let him pass by, bowed, "Excellency," and tried to continue but was blocked by the velvety mountain:

"What's this noise?"

"*Bueno*, I don't know either, Excellency, that's just what I'm going to find out, I'll be right back, it certainly is strange, isn't it? So loud!"

The Director of Armed and Unarmed Conservative Classes sniffed the air: "And this smell? The noise has lessened, but can't you smell something?" He frowned. "Nuisance! Smells, noises, and the telephone doesn't work, why isn't the telephone working? I need to get in touch with the Presidency, and I can't manage to, the phone is dead!"

"Dead? But I made dozens of calls early today . . . has your Excellency tried the one in the Blue Salon?"

"I'm just coming from there, it's dead too, damn nuisance! Get my chauffeur, see if the phone in my car is working, I have to make an urgent call."

"Be calm, Excellency, I'll take measures and come back at once, excuse me, will you?" said the young man, slipping away with a hurried bow. He continued down the steps, but stopped on the first flight.

"What's the meaning of this? Can you tell me what this is all about?"

Gasping for breath, in a torn apron and without his cap, the Chief Cook came running across the lobby. With an energetic motion, the young man went forward to meet him:

"How dare you come in here in this state!"

The man wiped the tomato sauce off his hands onto his chest. "A horrible thing has happened, sir, a horrible thing!"

"Don't shout, you're shouting, calm down"—and taking the Chief Cook by the arm, he pulled him into a corner. "Control yourself! Now, what happened? Without yelling, I don't want any hysterics, come on, calm down, what is it?"

"The lobsters, the chickens, the potatoes, they ate everything! Everything! There's not a grain of rice left in

the pans, they ate everything, and what they didn't have
time to eat they carried away!''

''But who ate everything, who?''

''The rats, sir, the rats!''

''Rats? . . . What rats?''

The Chief Cook took off his apron and rolled it up in his
hands. ''I'm leaving, I won't stay another minute, I think
they've taken over the world, by my mother's soul, I
almost died of fright when that cloud of them came through
the door, through the window, through the ceiling, they
practically carried me off and Euclidea too! They even ate
the dish towels, they only respected the refrigerator, it was
closed, but the kitchen is stripped bare! Stripped!''

''Are they still there?''

''No, they all went out squeaking like crazy, same way
they came in, I'd been hearing that noise for quite a while,
it sounded to me like a stream of water running strong
underneath the ground, then it pounded, whistled. Euclidea
was beating the mayonnaise, she thought she was seeing
ghosts when that quaking began, and at the same moment
they all came through the windows, the doors, there were
hordes of them everywhere you looked, like the end of the
world. And huge ones, see? As big as this. Euclidea
jumped up on the top of the stove, I jumped onto the table,
I even tried to grab back a chicken one of them was
making off with right under my nose, I pitched a jar of
tomato juice at him as hard as I could, and he put down
the chicken, reared up on his hind feet and faced up to me
like a man, by mother's soul, sir, he looked exactly like a
man dressed up as a rat!''

''My God, what—and the dinner?''

''Dinner? Did you say *dinner*, sir? There's not so much
as an onion left! Three of them upset the pot of lobsters
and spilled the lobster stew all over the floor, they had a
real party, I don't know how they didn't scald themselves
with the boiling water, God forbid, I'm getting out of here
right now!''

''Wait, calm down! And the servants? Do they know
about it?''

''Servants, sir? Servants? They're long gone by now,

nobody's crazy enough to stay here, and if I were them, I'd have taken off too, see? I wouldn't stay here even if you killed me!''

"Just a minute, wait! It's important to keep your head, do you understand? You go back there, open the canned goods, the cans are still there, aren't they? Wasn't the refrigerator closed? So there must be something left, fix a dinner with whatever you can, of course!''

"No, no! I wouldn't stay if you killed me!''

"Wait, I'm telling you, you will go back and carry out your orders, it's important that the guests don't find anything out, I'll take charge of this myself, understand? I'll go to the city immediately, bring back a supply of food and a squad of men armed to the teeth, we'll see if a miserable mouse can get into this house, we'll see!''

"But how will you go? Only if you walk, sir!''

The Chief of Public Relations pulled himself up short. His face was flushed with rage. He squeezed his eyes shut and made fists as if to pound the wall, but checked himself when he heard voices from the floor above. He hissed between his teeth. "Miserable cowards! You mean the servants took all the cars?''

"No, they ran away on foot, none of the cars work, José tried them one by one, see? The wires were chewed up, they ate the wires, too! You all can stay here, I'm going to hit the road and *now*!''

The young man slumped against the wall. His face was livid. "You mean that the telephone . . .'' he mumbled and fixed a motionless stare on the apron which the Chief Cook had left behind on the floor. The voices on the story above began to intermingle. A door slammed sharply. He shrank further into the corner when he heard his name: He was being called for, screamed for. He stared soundlessly, watching a slipper with leather edging pass by near the wadded-up apron on the carpet; the slipper glided by, its sole turned upward, as if it had little wheels or were being pulled by an invisible string. It was the last thing he saw because at that moment the entire house was shaken to its foundations. The lights went out. And then the invasion began, gushing thick as if a bag of rubber rocks had been dumped on top of the roof and were now bouncing everywhere in a thick inkiness of muscles, squeaks, and hundreds of blackest glittering eyes. When he felt the first bite rip off a piece of his trousers, he ran hunched-up across the floor, entered the kitchen with the rats hanging from his head, and opened the refrigerator. Groping for the shelves in the darkness, he tore them out, tossed the conserves into the air, fended off with a bottle two little eyes which were already heading for a dish of vegetables, and leaped inside. He closed the door but kept his finger in the crack so it wouldn't seal shut. When he felt the first needleprick on his unprotected fingertip, he substituted his tie for the finger.

During the rigorous inquiry that was made to clarify the events of that night, the Chief of Public Relations could never state exactly how long he must have stayed inside the refrigerator, rolled up like a fetus, the icy water dripping on his head, his hands stiffened with cramp, his mouth gasping at the tiny crack which from time to time a small snout would try to force open. He did remember, yes, a sudden silence which descended upon the great house: not a sound, not a movement. Nothing. He opened the refrigerator door and peered out. A tenuous ray of moonlight was the only presence in the ravaged kitchen. He went walking through the completely hollow house; neither furniture, curtains, nor rugs remained. Only the walls. And the darkness. Then there began a furtive, scratchy murmuring, which seemed to come from the Conference Room, and he had the intuition they were all together there, behind closed doors. He could not remember at all how he managed to get to the field, he would never be able to reconstruct his route, he ran for miles. When he looked back, the mansion was entirely illuminated.

The Consultation

Dr. Ramazian leaned over the windowsill and looked out at the garden bathed in the frail winter sun. A handful of patients were seated on the benches; others walked about, pallid and perplexed. An old man lay down on the grass, took off his pullover, threw it away from him. As he was starting to remove his woolen undershirt, the male nurse in jeans took him by the elbows and guided him inside. A young man in sandals quickly hid his face in his hands.

"Max! Maximilian!" the doctor called. "Can you come here a minute?"

The man who was watching the street through the wrought-iron gate turned around. He came up smiling, his hands thrust into the pockets of a navy-blue blazer with silver buttons. He bent over to take a dry leaf from his flannel trousers.

"Good afternoon, doctor."

The doctor knocked his already-empty pipe on the windowsill, blew at a flake of ash, and regarded the man.

"You're looking just fine to me, Max."

"I *am* just fine. And I had nightmares, doctor, I dreamed about a dove run over in the middle of the street, it had a green branch in its beak. The branch was so green in the middle of the blood, isn't that curious? The coincidence."

"What coincidence?"

"A kitten was run over right there in front of the gate. It was just like the dove."

"Without the green branch."

"Without the green branch," Maximilian repeated, staring at the pipe the doctor had left on the desk. "Are you going out?"

"I have an appointment, and Doris hasn't come yet. I wonder if you'd stay and answer the phone, would you do me the favor? I should be back before four."

"With pleasure," said Maximilian, leaning on the low windowsill. He jumped nimbly over it into the consulting room. "I'm delighted when you trust me at small jobs like answering the phone or cleaning your shoes."

The doctor closed the zipper of his briefcase.

"You never cleaned my shoes, Max."

"But I would. Yours and Jesus'."

"Jesus wore sandals," said Dr. Ramazian, clipping his pen to his pocket. He pointed to a pad of paper beside the telephone. "If there are any messages, write them down here, OK? You know where the coffee is if you want some. I won't be long."

When the doctor went out, Maximilian sat down on the swivel chair and propped his elbows up on the desk. He picked up the pipe and examined it attentively, sniffing the tobacco scent. He put it down, picked up the little metal spatula. The knock at the door was timid, constrained.

"Dr. Ramazian?" asked the new arrival, opening the door and peeking through the crack. He still held onto the handle. "Excuse me for barging in like this, my appointment was for four o'clock, but if you could see me now, can you see me now?"

"Yes, of course, come in. This is your first visit, isn't it?"

"Yes. I spoke to a Miss Doris but—"

"She didn't come today. Please sit down."

"It's just that I couldn't stand to wait," said the man, loosening his collar. He stroked his chin anxiously. "I didn't even shave, look there! I got here very early and tried to kill time walking around, but I felt so nervous, I think I'm on the verge of cracking up!"

"You exaggerate. People who are on the verge of cracking up don't say so. They don't even know it. Smoke?"

Maximilian asked, opening a cigarette box beside the pipe holder.

"Thanks, I prefer my own," the man said, taking them out of his pocket. His hand trembled. "I'm smoking three, four packs a day, I light each one on the flame of the one before, without stopping," he added, sweeping his eyes shiftily around and settling them on the window. "Are they all crazy? Those people out there."

"Not all, there are doctors and nurses mixed in with them. The design here is total freedom, we abolished the use of aprons, uniforms, the patients need to feel they are our equals. Even I can't tell them apart at times."

"My father used to know crazy people by their eyes."

Maximilian blinked his own and smiled.

"That's one element," he said, leaning over. He still held the cold pipe. "So?"

"I don't even know where to start, doctor, it's too absurd, ridiculous! This obsession, it makes no sense, so much fear, so much fear!"

"Fear of what, son?"

"Of death."

The white telephone on the desk rang softly, with the suppressed sound of a locust trapped in a drawer. Maximilian answered it, said, "Not here," made a move to pick up the pencil and after a resigned "As you wish," hung up. He took the pipe but refused the lighter which the other man offered him, he appreciated it but wasn't going to smoke, he was content just holding the pipe, full this way, as he was doing now. The man's expression became desolate.

"I would so much like to quit, doctor. Over three packs a day," he complained, resting his cigarette in the ashtray. Vehemently he wrung his thin fingers together. "I can't sleep, can't eat, can't fulfill my obligations, can't do anything except think about this, I can't even say the word or hear it without feeing bad, just now, don't you see? I started talking and right away I broke out in a sweat, this awful anxiety came over me! All the time thinking, thinking, I've lost my appetite to live. At my job, at home with my wife, in bed with my mistress, I have a mistress, such a sweet girl, I don't know how she can still put up with me, I've started to shy away from seeing her, the last time was a fiasco, in the middle, doctor, I stopped right in the middle like an old man, I went limp right there on top of her, or underneath. I forget which—it seems centuries ago! Centuries," he repeated, shaking his head. He dragged deeply on the cigarette, closing his congested eyes. "Today my wife had to remind me to change my clothes, I forget to shave, I'm exhausted, exhausted! Almost a year in this agony, doctor. It started slowly, with a certain uneasiness when they would advise me that someone had di—had packed up, I avoided the subject, detoured cemeteries, hospitals, anywhere I could smell it from far away, the thing, disinfected, covered up but present, active, do you understand? Until the uneasiness grew, turned to nausea, panic. I get up thinking that it could happen not only to me, but to the people I love, I look at my sons, I have two sons who are already laughing at me, at my fear of contagion, accidents, I think everything leads galloping to it, I feel like I've had all the diseases in the world! I had dozens of exams made, X rays, my doctor won't even let me in his door, 'there's nothing wrong with you!' he's told me countless times. And everything's wrong with me. The fear when I go to bed, that it'll get me when I'm asleep, red-handed, at times I imagine it with the face of a shameless old whore, brassy, jeering at me with her ancient eyes. At other times when I listen to music—my only consolation is music, doctor—at these times it seems ethereal, soft, like the virgins in ballads, crowned with a wreath of jasmine, beckoning to me with her ether-cold fingers . . . I don't know which of the two frightens me more, this one or the other, obscene rotten one. Ah, doctor, a thirty-five-year-old man trembling all over like a little child lost in the dark, whimpering, crying for its mother . . ." He leaned back in the chair, relaxing. "I cried for mine last night, when I was dreaming. She came, so affectionate, stretched her hand out to me but when I felt it in mine, limp and moist, green, I remembered she was already—I mean, I remembered, understand? and fled in terror. Just like I fled from my older brother when he had the stroke that carried him off. Do you believe I caught a plane to Rio half an hour after they notified me that he had . . . ? I invented the trip just so as to avoid seeing, I pretended to be indifferent, apathetic, my sister-in-law won't even speak to me, she despises me but how can I explain to her what's happening, how can she understand? Is she going to believe that I arrived in a hotel in Rio, locked myself in a room, and stayed there crying. We were very close, my brother and I.''

"I used to love my younger brother very much too, he was run over right here in front of the gates of the clinic.''

"Here in front, doctor?''

"Yes. But please continue.''

The man blew some ashes off his lapel, put out his cigarette. He stared at his nicotine-stained fingertips.

"Well, that's how it is, doctor, I can't go on running away, and where is there to run if it's everywhere. In the papers, the street, on television, in the market, at parties—it's inside the house. Inside me. It's principally inside me, my own prisoner. I don't read the papers anymore, don't go to the movies or the theater, the themes are all centered on it, I can't stand it. The only thing that could get my mind off it was the erotic magazines, with nude girls, there at least I couldn't find the slightest suggestion, you know? So much energy, so much sex. So much desire to use this sex. But little by little I started to sense, beneath so much youth and beauty, the seed of the thing hidden down at the bottom. At their peak today, but what about tomorrow?''

"Plato would offer us the metaphor of the apple. But continue, Mr. Guiterrez, continue.''

"One morning I woke up without any fear whatsoever, it had dissolved, and I was so stupid, I even thought I had freed myself from it when gradually I began to be scared of not being scared, do you understand? The emptiness seemed worse than anything, this space that the fear used to occupy. So then I wanted to test myself, to know if I were really free or not; I went marching into a ceme—into one of those gardens of rest, before I wouldn't go close to one even if you dragged me by the hair. I went on until I came to a curve in the roadway and noticed a . . . a ceremony, you know what I mean, doctor, even before I saw it I could already smell the thing, my sense of smell was supersharp, I can smell it miles away. It was all it took to make me start vomiting right there behind a cypress tree. I ran off like the wind, I only came to myself at home, sopping with sweat. Green with fear. Or yellow?" he asked, smiling weakly. He looked his own hands. "The color of fear. 'Take a leave of absence,' my boss advised, I'm a public employee, 'If you're sick, get a doctor's report and go for a trip, amuse yourself.' He wanted to help, everyone wants to help. But what was I to tell the doctors at the institute? If fear is my problem, how can I confess to them that I'm sick with fear? Everything in order. And this disorder, this anguish. It would be better to go crazy, the other night I thought quite a lot about this, it would be a solution. But I'm not going to go crazy, I'm going to—"

"Die."

"Don't say it, doctor, don't say it, just hearing it, see?" he murmured, wiping his forehead and chin with a handkerchief. He lighted a cigarette and sighed, "I warned you it was a ridiculous, absurd story, didn't I? When I was coming here today, a cortege, you know, cut in front of my taxi. Just seeing all those cars following the principal car made me so nervous I got out, changed streets, but do you think it did any good? Right away I ran up against a headline in a paper, the boy opened the paper right in my face, I had hardly turned away when the voice of another newsboy farther announced the tragedy, a bus that fell off a cliff, dozens of fatal injuries . . . I went into a café, and the conversation there was about an American convict who wants, who demands that they . . . that they execute him. But is that all they talk about? Or were they talking all the time before, and I just didn't notice? I don't know. I know that I want to isolate myself, to disappear to a place where this presence isn't so important, but does such a place exist? Convents are solitary, cut off. There, neither life nor antilife matter, one wouldn't expect them to worry about our . . . finitude. But they do, they want to gain saintliness through self-punishment, flagellation, in which is the memory of that thing exalted in prayers, hymns, images, repeated even in the greetings, 'Remember the . . . ?' you know, there's a community that greets each other that way, the minute they wake up, one sees another, smiles and says, 'Remember the . . .' ah! Ah. Why take away the joy of life while it lasts?''

Maximilian stared at the pipe closed inside the cup of his hand.

"I'm going to tell you a story, Mr. Guiterrez. I'll be brief.''

"Fernandes, doctor. Samuel Fernandes.''

"Pardon me. All the horror you have for this, let us say, fatality, a patient of mine had for automobiles. For the machine. He started the same way, like you did, manifesting in the beginning a certain dislike of driving, sold his car. He complained of the traffic, of other drivers. His dislike became aggravated, he got aggressive, easily frightened, his fear of entering a car growing so intense that he only got around by walking, distrustful, shunning the busier streets, his ears plugged with cotton to shut out the noise of the horns, panicking if a car got too close. Well, our city has a good many cars, which means he lived in a constant state of distress. When his vacation came (he was a bank clerk), he would run hysterically off to the country or the seashore, but seashore and country have all been invaded, the automobile is everywhere, like God. Where to flee? He tried to adapt, to dominate his horror. He couldn't. When he decided to consult me, he resembled a cadaver—excuse me, he was totally run-down. He confessed almost in tears: The phobia was becoming insupportable. This repugnance you have for the opposite of life, the special smell you notice when this opposite approaches, he felt the same thing when he smelled gasoline, oil, the black exhaust from the motor—he could smell it even locked inside a closet, even hidden under the bed. So I ordered him to get a job in an auto factory immediately.''

"An auto factory?''

"I can see you're surprised, Mr. Guiterrez, but it's no news that the only way to counteract poison is by using the poison itself. How do you cure snakebite? Eh? And what is homeopathic science? Get a job in an auto factory, I prescribed. And the fellow who couldn't even go near a garage or a car, went into the heart of them, was obliged to work with the parts, putting them together, taking them apart, tightening screws, painting, his head stuck inside the machine, his ears saturated with the sound of it. Early in the morning he would go and tinker with the motors, his nails black with grease; I saw his nails, neither soap nor scrub brush could clean the detestable presence from them. I taught him that one has to destroy one's ghosts by going to meet them, unmasking them, my dear boy, do you know what unmasking is? It's lifting the veil and looking the thing in the eyes. In the eyes.''

The telephone rang, and this time Maximilian scribbled a few notes before informing the caller that the person in question would be absent from the clinic for a few hours. He turned back to the man who waited, anxious, the cigarette hanging from the corner of his mouth, his restive hands open on his knees. He examined him in a cordial silence, tranquil.

''Did he get well, doctor?''

''Who?''

''The fellow . . .''

''Oh. Definitely. Once the worst phase of suffering was past, he began to take an interest in his work. He would come to see me three times a week, I never thought the adaptation process would be so fast; a month later he had already bought a car. And he would read automotive magazines, he helped to build the Engine Room display, collaborated with the magazine *Eight Wheels*, told anecdotes about the traffic, turned into an expert. During this period, he had only one relapse when he went, all smug, to see a film about auto racing and suddenly, in the middle of it, jumped up screaming and ran out terrified, all the old horror erupting so violently that I thought, uh-oh, there, back to zero. But no, the next day he was normal, everything OK. He went from being an admirer of the machine to being a lover, oh, the passion I have for this, he told me once, stroking a fender as one would stroke a woman's thigh. But his passion for the automobile wasn't to remain just passion—very soon he identified himself completely with the object.''

"I don't understand, doctor."

"Very simple, Guiterrez. He assumed the role of the automobile. He turned into an automobile, and so fervently that one morning he drank some high-octane gasoline and went buzzing down the street, brum, brum, brum, brrrruuuummmmm! He lost to a semi truck that was coming in the opposite direction."

"Did he die?"

"Just that. And now you dropped the word so naturally, see? There, you're on the way to a cure, to assume the role of the ghosts, better yet, to become one of them."

"Then he wasn't cured, doctor."

Caressingly, Maximilian passed the cold pipe back and forth on his smiling lip.

"But what do you call a cure? Would you by chance have wanted him to go on being a car for the rest of his life? You, for example, do you want to continue in panic like this up to the end? Is that what you want? Answer me! Do you want to suffer from this fear until you die from it?''

"No, doctor, that's not what I want, I don't ever want to be afraid again, ever!"

"I could recommend that you work as a nurse in a hospital—the kind where the patient goes in without the green leaf in his beak—" He laughed. And became serious, looking at his wristwatch: "It would be the same kind of treatment as in that case; hospitals are corpse factories, those who don't die of the disease they went in with catch another while they're there, you'd have first-rate material. But I want you to skip that phase, no point in stalling about, especially since you won't have another appointment, this is the last one."

"The last one?"

"It would be a sheer waste of time, son. Why go the long way round to arrive at the same objective? In the hospital you would become accustomed to—may I say the word? to death, and in such a way that you would end up forming an affection for the idea. You would go from being a simple admirer to being a lover of it, just like the fellow with the automobile, mounting it all day long, that same itch to unite with it. But that wouldn't be the end of it, the identification would be so profound that eventually you'd want to kill yourself. So therefore, better that you kill yourself now.''

''Doctor!''

''Immediately. Go out and kill yourself, that's an order.''

The man jumped up, somersaulting. He let his cigarette drop into the ashtray and stood there, his mouth half-open, his white face pouring sweat.

''Are you speaking seriously, doctor?''

''I've never been so serious in my life. You can only cure the fear of death with death itself. Kill yourself. Don't you want to be free? So I order liberation, you're saved, kill yourself,'' said Maximilian, fixing the man with a direct stare. ''Go out and kill yourself at once. A happy death to you.''

''But, doctor, wait . . . !''

Gently but firmly, Maximilian impelled the man toward the door.

''Obey. And now, good-bye.''

As soon as he was alone, he went to the window and through it watched the man cross the garden hesitantly, his hands open, swinging. He turned around once more, his terrified face contracting completely in the question mark of somebody who has forgotten to say—or do—something, what?

When Dr. Ramazian returned, Max was standing beside the table with the notepad in his hand. The pipe was empty, the ashtray clean.

''Right, Max. You can go have your snack now. Any messages?''

''A lady telephoned but didn't want to leave her name. And a patient, a Dr. Nóbrega, called also, he said he can only come on Friday, he'll set up the time with Doris.''

Dr. Ramazian filled his pipe. After puffing on it, he spoke.

"Fine, anything else? Did anyone come to see me?"

"Just a moment, let me see," said Maximilian, frowning. "No, nobody. Nobody. May I go?"

"Yes, of course," said the doctor, his eye wandering distractedly over the pad with its notations. "Fine, Max. You're getting along very well, you've made progress. I'm very pleased."

"Me too."

"There's only one last step, you know, to assume your role without possibility of going back. Then you will be cured."

Maximilian smiled. His voice was almost a whisper.

"Cured and screwed."

"What? Did you say something?"

"No, doctor. Nothing. You're quite right. Shall we go get something to eat?"

Yellow Nocturne

I saw the stars. But I didn't see the moon, although its milky luminosity spilled over the highway. I picked up a stone and squeezed it in my hand. Where could the moon be? I asked. Fernando, extremely impatient, tore off his coat and asked in a screeching voice if I intended to stand there like a statue all night while he had to fill the tank in the goddamn dark because *nobody* would pass him the flashlight. I bent inside the car whose door hung open, another way he had of showing his temper was leaving drawers and doors hanging open. Which I would go around closing in silence, with equal or greater hatred. I looked at the clock on the dash.

"Where's the flashlight?"

"Well, where would a flashlight be if not in the glove box, has the princess forgotten?"

Through the glass, the biggest star (Venus?) throbbed with blue reflections. I would like to be in a spaceship but with the motor turned off, soundless, without anything. Quiet. Or in this silent car, but without him. For some time already I've wanted to be without him, even with the problem of running out of gas.

"Things would be easier if you weren't so gross," I said, half-opening my hand and testing the flashlight on the white stone.

"All right, princess, if it isn't too *very* much trouble, do you think you could hand me the flashlight?"

When I remember this night (and I always am) I see

myself divided into two moments: before and after. Before, the little words, the little gestures, the little love affairs culminating in this Fernando, a mediocre adventure of short pleasure and long familiarity. If only he wouldn't use that tone of voice to ask if by chance anybody had taken his pen. If by chance anybody had thought to buy some new dental floss, this one was almost gone. It isn't, I answered, it's just that it got tangled up inside, if one takes off this plaque (I tried to lift it up) one can see that the spool is all there, but tangled, and when it gets tangled up that way, it's all over. Better throw it away and start something different. I didn't. Years and years trying to untangle the impossible thread, fear of loneliness? Fear of finding myself, the self I was so ardently searching for?

"Lady-of-the-Night," I said, breathing in openmouthed the perfume suddenly brought by the night wind. "And it's coming from over there."

"If the dinner's no good, I swear I'll upset the table," he said with his false calm. He uncapped the gasoline can. "I'm in the mood to eat fish, do you think there'll be fish?"

The sound of the thin stream of gasoline falling into the tank. The small noises coming from the earth. I went walking in the direction of *over there*, drawn by the perfume which now became denser as I became lighter. Now I was almost running along the side of the road, the fringed ends of my shawl opening like wings. I folded them over my chest and crossed the strip of ground vine that bordered the road, the hem of my dress catching on the dry twigs; I could have lifted it up but it was exciting to feel myself delicately held back by the cockleburrs (weren't they cockleburrs?), which I ended up taking along with me. I followed the path. So familiar, like the house just ahead there, the high white house outside of time but inside the garden. The intense perfume that had served to guide me was diluted now as if—its duty done—it were relaxing as it faded, may I? The stars seemed bigger in this night within a night. Feeling very natural, I opened the gate, the hinges beneath the layer of rust greeting me with their old squeak of aching teeth, come in at once, girl, come in! The foliage completely still. A light came on in the upper story of the house, then another. On the lower floor, three windows in succession projected their yellow torches as far as the porch; on the red brick columns the pale white flowers of the creepers seemed to be made of a phosphorescent substance. Then Ifigênia appeared in the main door, her apron clear-cut against the black of her dress. She brought her hands to her face in childlike joy, and turned to call inside:

"It's Miss Laurinha! How good you came back, Miss Laurinha!"

I hugged her. She smelled of cake.

"Cornmeal cake?"

"Of course," she said, examining me. She had come out onto the driveway to meet me and now paused to see me better. "You're wearing a new dress, isn't it new?"

I took her arm. She walked with difficulty, her short legs swollen. We stopped for an instant on the porch and without knowing why (which I didn't at the time) I avoided exposing myself to the light of the window. I pulled her closer to me.

"Are they all there?"

She answered in the same secretive tone.

"All but Rodrigo."

I leaned against the pillar. "But isn't he in the sanatorium?"

"He got out two weeks ago, didn't you know? But don't worry, Miss Laurinha, he's better now, he's changed so much," she said and took up the corner of my shawl, examining the weave more by means of her fingers than through the thick lenses of her glasses.

"I think this is the same stitch I used to make the wrap for Grandmother, remember? Only I used heavier wool. White shawls are beautiful, I made one for Miss Eduarda with silk thread."

I interrupted her meandering, but what about Rodrigo? The doctors had said he would have to stay there at least six months—wasn't that what they said? Had he run away? Did he run away, Ifigênia? Now she wrapped the shawl around my shoulder, and her gesture was the same one with which she used to wrap the sock soaked in alcohol around my neck, a sure cure for a sore throat, but don't move around, girl, oh! my father's green sock. But wait, Rodrigo; he'd stopped drinking, then?

"Completely. And he's even-tempered, do you remember how he used to shout when he talked? Now he speaks softly, he's really changed. I even think he's cured," she said, squinting to see me. She found my short hair strange, she liked it shoulder-length better, why did you have it cut, Miss Laurinha, why?

"Because I'm not a young girl anymore."

She smiled, interested in the shawl again, I must have paid a fortune for it, why hadn't I asked her to make it? She drew me inside the house; she had built a fire of very dry kindling in the fireplace, it was such a clean fire.

"And he didn't try again, Ifigênia? Answer me, he didn't try again?"

"No, Miss Laurinha, he didn't try again, nor will he, God is great, such a good boy."

The vestibule with its walls covered in faded beige paper sprinkled with pallid roses. The portrait of Pedro I in its heavy frame of worn gilt, encircled by pictures of severe men and rigid ladies in their black taffetas, the patterns of the woodworms advancing audaciously onto the lace collar of my Portuguese ancestress up to the edge of her sepia-colored chin. The glass case full of porcelain and jade bibelots. The wide runner of red velvet along the hallway, silent bridge offering to lead me to the essence—of what?

"And there are cornstarch biscuits, too, the ones you like," announced Ifigênia, taking my shawl. She folded it over her arm with a mellifluous gesture. "I'm always thinking about doing what other people want, but other people never think about doing what I want. There's something I want so much, asked for so many times, I wonder if you still remember?"

I put my arm around her, yes, I remembered, the trip! I had promised to take her to Aparecida by car, she wanted to fulfill a vow and so I had offered to drive her, let me take you. I didn't. But it wasn't out of meanness, Ifigênia, it's just that I kept putting it off, putting it off, and ended up forgetting, will you forgive me?

"Forgive what?" I heard somebody ask behind me, Ducha?

She liked to come up stealthily that way, on tiptoe in her slippers the same color as the wallpaper. I noted that her bustline continued timid beneath the black ballet leotard and her waistline was still straight like a little girl's, thirteen years old? She kissed me in her polished way, affecting indifference. I had to contain myself so as not to pull her by the hair, you little silly, you little silly!

"Your sister promised to drive me to Aparecida, and to this day I'm still waiting," said Ifigênia. She stroked the shawl folded over her arm as one strokes a cat. "If I'd known, I would have taken the bus."

Ducha struck the pose of a ballerina at rest. She looked up at the ceiling.

"She made me a promise she didn't keep, too, it was to trade my yellow sweater for the big mirror, that one with a cupid, I really needed a mirror to practice in my room and what happened? My dear sister kept the sweater, yes, ma'am, first thing tomorrow I'll bring the mirror, she promised. And did she? I continue to practice"—she covered her eyes pretending to cry—"with a tiny little mirror this size!"

I wanted to hug her, and she moved aside, I wasn't to disarrange her sprayed hair, caught at her neck with a barrette, no sentimentalities, what I want is my mirror! she seemed to say to me with an ironic smile and my heart spilled over with happiness, pain; her black leotard retained the scent of the deep wardrobes with their little bags of dried aromatic plants. The past mingled with the future, which now came to me in the warm smell of the fireplace. Or of the candles? I blew them out, no, no, candles, listen, Ducha, I swear I'll bring it tomorrow for sure, for sure! Do you believe me?

"Shh!" she ordered, I must be quiet, because in the parlor Grandmother had decided on a Chopin waltz.

"Ducha," I began and didn't manage to say any more. She straightened her body, lifted her head, and forgetting me, the mirror, everything, she proceeded diaphanous down the corridor, I am an artist! expressed in every disdainful, inspired movement. An artist!

"She looks like a little fairy godmother," sighed Ifigênia as she encircled my waist and conducted me along the red carpet.

I could still hear my frightened heartbeats, so loud that I turned toward Ifigênia, had she heard? But there was the piano. And the voices which already reached us, we were halfway down the corridor. With the tips of my fingers I lightly stroked the arm of the bench, its wood as smooth as satin, a swan's neck rolling up in a soft curve until it descended and buried the tip of its beak in the wing feathers carved in the side of the seat. To one side, another china cabinet of bibelots, with the little porcelain cups as fine as eggshell, the famous miniature service, my life's passion. Don't touch! Grandmother would scold, this isn't for children to play with, you're going to break every-thing. I didn't break anything, I swallowed a little teapot, I used to like to fill my mouth with the pieces which I would then spit out onto the dolls' tea table. I could feel the teapot again as a lump rose in my throat.

"I'm so happy, Ifigênia."

"Then why are you crying?"

Quickly I dried my eyes on the hem of her apron and drew back, wasn't it strange? On the spotless cambric there was no sign of my makeup, just the clean dampness of the tears. I couldn't tell which eyes had cried, the present ones or those of another time.

The parlor seemed to throb beneath the reflection of the strong fire in the fireplace, which tinged the mirrors with red. The chandelier. I saw Grandfather in his high-backed chair, playing chess with Eduarda's professor, wasn't he Eduarda's professor? Eduarda found a German teacher who is a doll!—Ducha had announced to me. You mean the German doll is on such intimate terms? I wanted to ask but Eduarda didn't see me, she was busy preparing some-thing to drink at the table set up in the back of the room. She had a flower in her hair, a sign of happiness, are you in love, Eduarda? I saw Grandmother—the dear, the

dear!—in the dress she wore for special occasions, her
head bent over the keyboard, accelerating the rhythm to
accompany Ducha who whirled in a ring of steps around
the piano. I saw Ifigeñia with her short walk, her short
breath, arranging the glasses on the table, it was punch
Eduarda was fixing. And I saw myself, so much older yet
still retaining an ambiguous innocence, sufficient to behave
spontaneously in the company of the right guests. Some
element or other that I already had, or was later to have,
warned me that this old evening was new. I walked around
Grandfather's chair and hugged him from behind. He greeted
me, lifting in his hand the rook he was about to move.

"Do you know this granddaughter of mine, professor?
The intellectual of the tribe, eh, girl?"

The German (he was taller than I had supposed) remembered that we had already been introduced and smiled
rather maliciously, half-amused. Eduarda had told him a
lot about me. I looked at him questioningly, suspicious,
but his penetrating stare made me drop my eyes. He turned
back to Grandfather, who was still holding the rook.

"It's your turn."

Then Eduarda saw me and came bringing a glass of
punch. She looked so young with her loose hair and her
face bare of makeup that I was as disturbed as if I had seen
myself approaching in a sudden flash of youth. She kissed
me quickly and handed me a glass, here, try it, I think I
put in too much sugar, isn't it too sweet? I saw that
Grandmother was calling me to sit beside her on the piano
bench and also noticed, behind the piano, the big clock
which said nine o'clock. In the glass, the punch with a
pitted cherry, exposed, floating on the purple surface.

"Come on, drink it, it's not poisonous," ordered Eduarda,
and her laugh was so confident that I thought it unjust for
time to continue, and wanted to run and grab the pendulum, stop! I drained the glass, biting the crystallized cherry
between my teeth, along with other bits of fruit I couldn't
identify, Eduarda kept the mystery of the ingredients to
herself.

"Be careful, Grandfather!" I said. "You're going to
lose that knight!" Eduarda's suitor winked at her:

"It's already lost."

Grandfather looked at the knight. Looked at me. And shaking his hand, he affected an anger he was far from feeling as he accused me of cheating during our last game, you did cheat, yes, ma'am, do you think I don't know? You took advantage when I went to get my sweater and moved the castle that was defending my queen, I would never have lost the way I did!

"You stole Grandfather's castle! You stole Grandfather's castle," yelled Ducha, jumping toward us and back again, horrified, her arms open and body curved as if she were bent by a strong wind. "You kept my mirror and Grandfather's castle!"

"Worse than stealing a castle is stealing your cousin's fiancé," whispered Eduarda, pulling me by the hand.

We went closer to the window. Her eyes were deep purple like the punch. I closed mine, Eduarda, I wanted so much to explain this to you and didn't have the courage, but now listen, he said you'd broken off, that it was all over."

"He did?"

"It wasn't my fault, Eduarda, when we started going out I was certain you two were no longer together, that you weren't in love anymore, I didn't feel I was betraying anyone."

"No?"

I saw the stars shining close. Close the perfume of the night which took me and brought me back whole. Genuine. I faced Eduarda, really faced her for the first time, but was it necessary to say anything? Was it really necessary?

We looked at each other, and now my thoughts were a current flowing from my hands to hers, we were holding hands; yes, I was jealous, insecure, I wanted to assert myself, and all I got was disappointment, suffering. There was Rodrigo (my God, Rodrigo) who was my own dear love, a tumultuous love, all improvisation, madness, but love. And I thought it would be the opportunity to free myself from him, it was an advantageous trade, but I miscalculated, even in the first meetings I discovered that betrayal makes love go rotten. You were present everywhere, Eduarda, in the street, in restaurants, in the movies, in bed—one day I could actually feel you breathing. It became so insupportable that the last time, when he went into a sound compartment to listen to a record, I couldn't stand it, and I ran away, we were in a store buying records, I want to hear this one, he said, going into the glass compartment, wait for me a second. I went toward the front window, pretending to look for God knows what, and then I took advantage and ran off with my head down, without looking to either side. Eduarda, say you believe me, say you believe me!

Her eyes, which had been dark, slowly became transparent. Everything's all right now, Laura, we're together again—she seemed to say to me. We're together for always—and squeezed my hand tight. But she didn't let me get any more emotional, she got a cornmeal biscuit that Ifigênia offered and put it in my mouth, come on, you're too thin, you need to eat, don't be sad. I began to feel miserable: I did cheat Grandfather at chess, I said, but I choked on the biscuit, and Eduarda broke out laughing like she had at the dolls' tea party when I swallowed the teapot. Her bracelet—a band of gold—got caught on my dress. She tried to take it off her wrist, keep it, Laura, for our new alliance, you like these symbols. But the bracelet, already free of my dress, wouldn't come off her wrist; it was a solid ring that could only be removed over her hand, I'm fatter, see? I'm getting fat from happiness, I'm so happy with my German, isn't he beautiful? The fire in the fireplace was reflected in her cheeks, as in the chandelier, the mirror; I want to shout from so much love! She grabbed me, and we started to dance, laughing like two fools until we got to the piano, where she handed me over to Grandmother, stay here while I go rescue my love, Grandpa must be wanting to play another game, she said. And she became serious. She took my arm.

"Rodrigo won't be long."

"Who?" asked Grandmother, moving over to make room for me on the bench. "Who won't be long?"

"Rodrigo," said Ducha, opening her arms in a soft winglike movement and falling down on the big cushion.

When she bent over to tie the ribbon on her slipper, I saw the little boy lying on the rug. He was wearing pajamas and playing with a box of colored blocks, but had he been here when I arrived?

"You're thinner, Laurinha," lamented Grandmother, examining me affectionately but watchfully. And wasn't I perhaps too made up? She preferred me a thousand times without makeup, like Eduarda. And why was I trembling that way? You're freezing, girl, drink some tea—she ordered, getting me a cup. Was it because of him I was so tense? Because of (she pronounced the name in a hushed voice) Rodrigo?

Her coquettishly teased hair had highlights of a lilac-blue color which made me think of violets. Now she was trying to calm me in the same tone with which she used to say, at bedtime, that these ghost stories were nothing to be afraid of, all this was make-believe, dearie, now then, go to sleep. "Rodrigo? But he's cured now, don't worry anymore. I don't deny that it was a very serious crisis, but it's over. It's over. Just yesterday we were talking, he's thinking about taking up his studies again, he's already making plans—" she said, and I sensed in her look (or in mine?) something of reticence. For an instant she seemed to be composed of a damp lilac-blue cloth, the same color as her hair. "Don't go, wait!" I asked her, without knowing whether or not I was screaming. In the fireplace, the fire was lower.

"At times the fear comes back," I said.

"Fear of what, my dear? But aren't you in love? Then you need to be," she said, looking at my hands. No special ring? No special boyfriend? Well, Eduarda, who was my age (she hesitated, taking up her lorgnon again) —weren't we the same age? I always thought you two would synchronize because when Ivone was pregnant your mother also . . . (she began counting on her fingers but lost herself in the dates). "What I mean is, Eduarda found this fellow so quickly, everything went at a gallop. They're going to be married in December, isn't it wonderful?"

Her voice passed now onto another plane as she went into details: After the wedding they would go to Germany, his parents lived there, in a little city that had the most darling name, Ulm, but after the visit they would travel all through Europe during the long vacation period. Ducha was burning with desire to go along and enroll in a ballet course in Paris, that little slip of a girl, imagine! What she didn't like was this idea of an airplane, why did young people have this mania for airplanes? A steamship was so much better, ah, the delicious journeys by sea, she could still remember so well when she went with Grandfather to Italy in an Italian transatlantic liner, so many amusements on board, the games, the parties! But the best time of all was when she sat back in her deck chair, pulled her quilt up to her knees, and read a Conan Doyle novel. Or just sat looking at the sea.

"Do you suppose he still thinks about me?"

Grandmother took a while to answer. She made a quick movement, bringing the palms of her hands together, as if she were closing a book, who? Rodrigo? Yes, he did, but in a different way, without affliction or rancor, he was much changed after his attempt. If he could get away, go for a journey, but a journey at sea, in a steamer like that one, she didn't remember the name of the ship, wasn't it curious? But she had never forgotten the gulls. The wind.

"Where did he get the revolver?"

The word *revolver* fell into her lap like a gull. Or a fish. Startled, she shook the biscuit crumbs from her dress. With the corner of her handkerchief she cleaned a drop of tea from the keyboard, the revolver? Who knows? He had always been such a reserved boy, creating a private world all his own, he didn't let anyone else enter it.

"He invited me in, but I refused."

Ducha leaned on her elbows and came crawling across the carpet until she touched my shoe:

"How chic these gold heels are!" she said, and signaled for me to bend over, she wanted to whisper in my ear: "The bullet came within a fraction of an inch of his heart."

"They're going to be in for a very cold winter. If they went by steamship, they wouldn't notice the sudden change," sighed Grandmother. Enervated, she turned toward Ducha, who was pointing to the piano, I want to dance, play, play! "Wait, girl, even if you don't need an intermission, I do!"

I looked at the heavy curtains, at the china cupboard which seemed less brilliant to me beneath the light layer of dust. "Time doesn't touch you, I said. You're all the same, just the same."

"The piano's changed, dear," said Grandmother, smiling and striking a bass chord. "I had it tuned, do you remember how it used to be? And if you aren't aware of it, it's because you never come to visit me, I was sick, recovered, fell sick again, and not even a telephone call. Nothing. I could have died, and my granddaughter wouldn't even have known because she didn't ring up even once to find out how Grandmother was."

"Grandmother dear, you know very well how much I love you all. It's just that I've been truly out of touch, but you *do* know."

"I know, Laurinha, but I like proof, proof is important."

Ducha made a face:

"How ugly, Laura! Little Red Riding Hood went across a forest all full of wolves just to take the cake to her Granny who had a cold, didn't she have a cold?" She raised up onto her tiptoes, ready to dance. She had her little smile, "You didn't come to get Ifigênia, who wanted to keep her vow, you didn't deliver my mirror, you stole Grandfather's castle, took away Eduarda's fiancé, and didn't visit Grandmother."

"Ducha, dance, go on," motioned Grandmother. She began playing a slightly dissonant melody. Ragged. "There, go dance."

"And on top of it all, you play the *femme fatale*," added Ducha quickly, making the motions of grabbing a weapon and pointing it toward her chest. She pulled the trigger, "Bam! . . ." and went reeling, pretending to let go of the gun. She lay down on the big cushion, her right hand holding her chest, the other waving a feeble farewell. *"I would kill myself in March, if you resembled perishable things . . ."* she recited, out of breath. "Why March? Only H.H. knows, if the poet says March, it has to be

March . . ." (she drew back, her arms arched) *"March or April?"*

"She's a love of a girl, but a little tiring," murmured Grandmother, bending over to kiss me. "I wrote this music, do you like it? I'm going to call it *Yellow Nocturne*."

Even before I went nearer the fireplace, I sensed the fire reviving itself with a last effort. Ifigênia touched my arm as if she were going to offer me something:

"Rodrigo just arrived."

I hid my face in my hands but even so I could see him in front of me with his faded jeans and jacket with leather patches at the elbows. He took me by my wrists and uncovered my face. The coals of his eyes were burning but he had the same sweet smile as before. He waited. When I was able to speak, the ashes had completely covered the grate.

"I denied you, Rodrigo. I denied you and betrayed you, and I betrayed Eduarda. But I wanted you to know how much I loved you both."

He arranged my hair, lighted my cigarette. Laughed.

"If we don't betray those closest to us, who is there to betray?" (He became serious.) "We were very young."

Were? I raised my head. I didn't care now if he saw me face to face. I actually wanted to expose my devastation, did he know then? I heard my voice coming from far away.

"I spent the whole night apologizing, you were the only one left, Oh, God! How I needed to see you again," I said touching his chest.

He flinched. Then I remembered, but does it still hurt, Rodrigo? And do you still have to wear bandages? He took a glass of punch, made me drink it. I mustn't be impressed by this, he was just sensitive, and with sensitive people this is a very tender zone, the healing took a long time.

We didn't need to talk. Inside me (and him) there was now calm. Silence. I began to feel cold and went to get my shawl. When I came back, he was gone. Where's Rodrigo? I asked Ifigênia. She was leading the resistant little boy off by the hand, Rodrigo? But wasn't he with me just a minute ago?

"I know how to make animal faces, look, auntie," yelled the boy, sticking his fingers out from his forehead. "Look at the animal!"

Then everything happened very rapidly. Or was it slowly? I saw Grandfather go toward the door in the back of the parlor, pick up the key from the floor, open the door, put the key back in the same place, and leave, closing the door behind him. Then it was Grandmother's turn; she passed by me with her cane and her lorgnon, waved to me, and leaving the key in the same place, went after Grandfather. I saw Eduarda from a distance, helping her fiancé put on his coat, but where did they all go? I asked, and she didn't hear or didn't understand. They were laughing as they went toward the door. Ducha leaped between them, got the key, knelt on one knee, and placed the key on the other, bending with the reverence of a medieval page offering his services. I turned away, not wanting to see. Out of shame, I kept my back turned when Ifigênia went by dragging the child who wanted to play some more, you can't, love, no whining, be nice. The pyramid of colored blocks which he had built on the rug went tumbling down through my tears. When I could bear to look, the parlor was empty. I saw the chess game interrupted in the middle. The open piano (did she finish the *Nocturne*?) and the book on top of the mantel. The half-full teacup. Ducha's barrette forgotten on the big cushion. The pyramid. Why did objects (and projects) move me now more than people? I looked at the chandelier; it seemed as dark as the fireplace.

I went out the front door and even before going around to the back, I had guessed that behind the door through which they had all gone, there was nothing; only fields.

I crossed the garden which was no longer a garden without the gate. Without the perfume. The path (narrower, or was it my impression?) came out onto the road; the car was still there with its door open and headlights on. Fernando was closing the container.

"Did I take very long?"

He put on his coat and lit a cigarette, if I'd taken long? But what did I mean? Had I gone somewhere?

I got into the car and saw myself in the mirror illuminated by the flashlight. My makeup was intact.

"Do you know what time it is?"

"Nine on the dot. Why?" he asked, turning on the dashboard radio. He put a hand on my knee: "You're beautiful, my love, but so distant, so cold, eeh! What shitty music," he cried, changing the station. "Do you suppose the dinner will be any good? I'm in the mood to eat fish."

I stared at the Milky Way through the windshield, closing my eyes. I squeezed hard the bracelet I still held in my hand. "Isn't that a squirrel?" asked Fernando, pointing excitedly to the road. "There, see it?"

"It could be a rabbit."

"But rabbits don't come out at this hour."

Neither do squirrels, I said or thought of saying. But already he wasn't listening.

The Presence

When he went up the graveled entrance and parked the car in front of the hotel, the elderly couple who were walking on the grass retreated quickly and stared at him from a distance. The old porter who tended the reception desk also shrank momentarily back. He set his suitcase on the floor and asked for a room. For how long? He wasn't exactly sure, maybe about three weeks. Or more. The old man examined him from head to foot. He forced a paternal smile, disguising his alarm with an exaggerated cordiality, but did the young man want a room? Here, in *this* hotel? But it was an old people's hotel, almost all the guests were long-time permanent residents, what fun could a young man have in a hotel like that? After nine P.M., absolute silence because everyone went to bed very early. And the food was so insipid, no salt, dishes without the slightest imagination in keeping with strict diets—weren't they elderly? And elderly people have health problems, so many illnesses both real and imaginary: arthritis, chronic bronchitis, asthma, high blood pressure, phlebitis, emphysema, not to mention the more dramatic diseases, it was pointless to enumerate them all. Old age itself was a disease. A healthy young man spending his vacation in a hotel as cold as a hospital? In hospitals at least there was some hope for the patients to leave cured, but the disease of old age was incurable and aggravated by the passage of time. Unfair to offer him this picture of decadence which, in spite of being disguised (hospitals belonged to the bourgeoisie) was really too de-

48

pressing. The pleasure with which youth sees itself reflected in a mirror! But the old age concentrated there was so cruel that the mirrors had finally been removed. During the last redecoration, the ones which showed noticeable signs of decomposition, such as porous spots and yellowish borders, had been removed, the silver shrunken beneath the crystal like thin paper burning slowly. The larger mirrors of the dining room had been taken down at the same time, though they were still in good repair. Their replacement was never seen to, and the subject was dropped, who needed them? The relief of the guests, freed from those frozen witnesses that captured them from all angles, was evident; the smaller bathroom mirrors were more than sufficient, just the essential to shave, comb one's hair. A ridiculous touch of rouge. And the number of mirrors when the hotel was opened! (Would the young man care to hear more?) Well, it had been fifty years ago. At that time he was no more than a bellboy who helped with the luggage. The families would arrive in their cars bursting with suitcases, boxes, servants, children, bicycles. In the long summer vacations, the swimming pool (which was still there despite its cracks) used to buzz. The dances into the wee hours. The games. And the competitions on the tennis court, the horseback rides through the countryside—the hotel had offered an excellent stable. Carriages. But little by little the older guests began to dominate the clientele while the younger ones grew rarer, he couldn't explain why, but in fact the transformation, although slow, had been final. A museum-mausoleum. What young person could feel well in that kind of hotel? If he went a few kilometers farther down the same road by which he had come, he would find an excellent hotel, there were various arrows indicating the way, it was in a very pleasant wood. And from what he had heard, its atmosphere was cheerful. Congenial.

The young man took his identification cards from the pocket of his leather jacket and placed them on the marble counter: He wanted a room in this hotel, and he would only refrain from insisting if the regulations had some clause forbidding a young man of twenty-five to stay there.

The old porter ran his hesitant fingertips over the threadbare collar of his brownish uniform. He was no longer smiling as he examined the documents. He gave them back, his pale-blue eyes cold. Perhaps, just perhaps, he hadn't been sufficiently clear: The fact was that even if he didn't mind the old people, it was quite probable the old people would mind him—and how! So easy to understand, how was it a smart young man like himself failed to see? The old people formed a community with its own ways, customs. Here they had come together, and their antique fragility, so threatened beyond the gates, had been transformed into a force, a system. They were stubborn beings. In the secret battle to guarantee their survival, they had forgotten the world which had rejected them, and if they weren't happy, at least they had gained one thing: security. The right to die in peace. On the second floor of the hotel, for instance, lived a musical-comedy actress who had been very famous. Very much loved. Now reduced to a simple wreck, she had locked herself in her shell, terrified of the public's curiosity, of the realism of the press avid to photograph her in her loneliness, but what do you want with me? she screamed at the reporter who managed to ambush her and publish the photo with the headline that made her cry for two days. When the elevator broke down, she alone, who could still walk with a certain agility, continued on the second floor, the others were transferred to the first because of the stairs. On this floor there lived an old athletic idol who had gotten to two world Olympics. He lived in a wheelchair. And since he didn't read the papers or turn on the television (whoever wanted could have his own private set) he managed to forget that the race with the flaming torch was proceeding, glorious, without him. He forgot just as he had been forgotten. The medals and trophies which he couldn't bear to see in his first days of invalidism were now displayed on the shelf of his room, at times he looked at them but without the old emotion, they became an integral part of his senility, like his hot water bottle or wheelchair. The neighbor was an

arteriosclerotic businessman who in a short number of
years had regressed into his youth, then adolescence, and
now was becoming a child again. But a child protected
even by the most neurasthenic guest of all, a homosexual
who lived with an ancient cat. He had had a tragic experience in his youth: When his boyfriend tried to kill him,
everyone found out what he had tried desperately to hide;
they both came from important families and were very
well known. Today of course nobody cared, but back then
he had known only rejection and suffering. In this hotel he
had regained his equilibrium by watching the town ladies
who played patience open their cards in a taciturn exercise
of silence. By listening to the fat old maid play her banjo
punctually every Saturday. Rereading in the small library
(a few sparse worn-out volumes) *The Three Musketeers* or
The Count of Monte Cristo. But now a tenuous shadow
had fallen over their heads. Over their defenses. Now a
young man had come to stay. To remind them (and with
such emphasis!) of what all of them had lost: beauty, love.
A young man with teeth, muscles, and sex—no, one needn't
laugh, they had managed to forget this traditional measure
of the soundness of things. His mere presence would upset
everything, cause a revolution of memory. And the time
for revolution was past, nobody wanted to renew, only to
conserve. To guarantee this survival which in itself signi-
fied true heroism—the weaker had all died. These remained,
engaged in a battle the more terrible because it was on the
sly, they were sly—was he making himself clear? They
were not good.

He lighted a cigarette and offered one to the porter who
thanked him, he wasn't allowed to smoke. He looked at
the chandelier with its long tear-shaped crystal prisms
heavy with dust. He smiled as he pointed in the direction
of the small elevator, round and gold, "It's beautiful! It
looks like a cage!" and unzipped his leather jacket, it was
hot. The porter bent over the thick hotel registry, dipped
the pen in the inkwell but stopped with his hand poised in
the air. He arched his fatigued eyebrows: Didn't the gentleman understand that this would be an imposition? An
intrusion? He was like the right side of a fabric, they the

reverse side. Or was it the other way round? The problem was that he, a mere porter, wouldn't be the slightest help if the community should decide subtly upon his exclusion. Even foolish as these elderly people seemed, they guarded the secret of a wisdom that was sharpened on the whetstone of death. One must remember that they would use *all* their resources to ensure that the rules of the game be obeyed. How bitter could the hatred be for one who had come to humiliate them, ironic, provocative, upsetting the contest? The young man was animated with the idea of the swimming pool—but if in that same leaf-choked pool his beautiful body should appear floating as unconscious as the leaves? They would close the door quickly because of the current of wind, old people don't like drafts. And would go, satisfied, back to their concerns. To their little Sunday games, such happy Bingo, the cards being covered with kernels of corn while the announcer (no outsiders near?) sings out the numbers with his customary jokes, always the same because they enjoy repetition, like children: Number twenty-two, two ducks in the pond! Forty-four, a double door! Number three, it's time for tea! So playful, these old folks!

The young man laughed and took off his dark glasses, his face lighting up. He had golden specks in the bottom of his pupils. Did the porter by any chance read detective stories? Those novels by the little old Englishwoman? Oh, he preferred crossword puzzles. He picked up his suitcase. If possible, an apartment on the second floor. Dinner was at seven, wasn't it? Fine, he had time for a good swim, it was a delightful afternoon. No problem that the pool was deserted, wasn't the water fresh? He only asked to have a little ice brought to him, he liked to sip a drink in the pool. No, whiskey wasn't necessary, he had brought his own brand.

A little old lady with a lilac-colored lace collar crossed the lobby in her wheelchair pushed by a calm nurse in a cap; she was gesticulating, angry, muttering between her hard gums while the other followed after her, shaking her head and smiling, "Poor darling! She's a bit irritable today, but then, at eighty-nine! . . . poor, poor darling . . ."

The new arrival bowed low in their direction and turned
back to the porter who showed his opaque dentures in a
constrained smile. So he really meant to insist on staying?
Well, there was a very sunny room on the second floor,
facing the swimming pool. "I hope you'll be satisfied,
sir," he added as he waved to an old man wearing a
knee-length apron, please, would he conduct the new guest?
The young man bounded up the red velvet steps with wide
leaps, and waited for the employee at the top, holding the
suitcase which the old man tried in vain to carry. When he
entered the apartment, followed by the old man with his
ring of keys, he sniffed with an expression of pleasure the
stale perfume which seemed to come from the old-fashioned
furniture, lavender? And asked as he opened the bag if
there were any ghosts about, he had always dreamed of a
hotel with ghosts. We are the ghosts, answered the old
man, and he laughed out loud. He took out his bottle of
whiskey and turned on the record player.

When he climbed up on the diving board, he noticed a
figure peering out through the lace curtain of one of the
windows. Amused, he looked down at the deep green
water, where the leaves floated in calm waves. He opened
his arms, dived. As he swam on his back, he saw a white
head in the crack of the window on the first floor. Then
another head, a man's, appeared and remained a little
behind, in shadow. A vague shred of argument reached
him before the window was slammed shut. He stretched
out on the stone bench and let his arms hang down, his
red trunks dripping water, his eyes closed. His fingertips
caressed his chest where the sun-bleached hairs were already beginning to dry. He laughed silently as he picked
up the glass he had left on the ground; his movements
were fragmented in slow-motion, calculated. At dinner,
even before trying the food, he sprinkled it with salt,
pepper, and Worcestershire sauce, and applauded vigorously for the three old musicians (a pianist, a violinist, and
a bald bass fiddle player) who played old songs to which
the sparse guests who came down to dine listened imper-

turbably. He thought the guava paste with cheese tasted slightly bitter.

Upon going to bed, after drinking the nightcap served at nine o'clock, he was already feeling poorly.

The Touch on the Shoulder

The man found it strange, that greenish-gray sky with a waxy moon crowned by a thin tree branch, the leaves outlined in minute detail against the opaque background. Was it a moon or a darkened sun? It was difficult to know if night was falling or if it was already morning in this garden, which had a dull luminosity like that of an old copper coin. The perfume of the herbs was strange. And the silence, crystallized as if in a painting, with a man (himself) as part of the scenery. He went walking down the path carpeted with leaves the color of burning cinders, but it wasn't autumn. Nor spring because the flowers didn't have that sweet breath that announces butterflies, he didn't see any butterflies. Nor birds. He opened his hand against the live but cold trunk of the fig tree, a trunk without ants or resin, he didn't know why he expected to find resin glazed in the cracks, it wasn't summer. Nor winter, although the slimy coolness of the rocks made him think of the overcoat he had left on a hanger in his office. A garden outside of time, but inside my time, he thought.

The humus which rose from the ground filled him with the same torpor as the landscape. He felt hollow, the sensation of lightness mingling with the unsettling feeling of being without roots; if his veins were opened, nothing would come out, not even one drop of blood. He picked up a leaf. But what garden was this? He had never been there before, and he didn't know how he had found it. But he knew without a doubt that this routine had been broken because something was going to happen, what? He felt his heart pounding. He was so habituated to a daily life without anything unexpected, any mysteries. And now, this insane garden blocking his way. With statues yet, wasn't that a statue?

He went up to the young woman of marble who was gracefully raising her skirts so as not to dampen them or her bare feet. A frightfully useless young woman in the middle of a dry fountain, stepping carefully, choosing among the rocks mounted around her. But the cracks between the toes of her delicate feet showed the corrosion of an era when the water had lapped around them. A black streak descended from the top of her head, ran down her cheek, and lost itself as it curved between her breasts, half-revealed by a loose bodice. He noticed that the streak had marked her face more deeply, devouring the left side of her nose, but why had the rain chosen that course to concentrate its obstinate dripping? He stared at the curly head, the ringlets of hair hanging over the base of the neck which seemed to invite a caress. Give me your hand, I'll help you, he said and shrank back; a hairy insect, wound up in a spiderweb, crawled out of her small ear.

He let the dry leaf fall, thrust his hands into his pockets, and went on, stepping with the same caution as the statue. He walked around a clump of begonias, hesitated between two cypresses (but what did that statue mean?) and went on down a path that seemed less somber. An innocent garden. And unsettling as the puzzle games his father used to enjoy playing with him: In the careful drawing of a forest there was a hunter hidden, he had to find it quickly so as not to lose the game. Come on, son, look in the clouds, in the tree, isn't he dressed in the leaves of that branch? On the ground, doesn't the curve of the stream form a cap?

He's on the steps, he answered. This singularly familiar hunter who would come up from behind, in the direction of the stone bench where he was going to sit, just ahead there. So as not to take me by surprise (he detested surprises) he will discreetly make some sign before putting his hand on my shoulder. Then I'll turn around to see. He stopped short. The revelation made him stagger, faint with dizziness: Now he knew. He closed his eyes, covered his face, and doubled up, almost touching his knees to the ground. It would be like a leaf falling on his shoulder but if he looked back, if he obeyed the call . . . He straightened his body, smoothed his hair. He felt observed by the garden, judged even by the rosebush with its little roses smiling shyly just ahead. Then he felt ashamed. My God, he murmured, in the tone of one who excuses himself for having panicked so easily, my God, what a miserable way to act, what if it were a friend? He began to whistle, and the first notes of the melody transported him back to the little boy in his uniform from Senhor dos Passos in the Good Friday Procession. The image of Christ grew larger in its glass coffin, wavering suspended above the heads, lift me up, Mama, I want to see! But He was still too high, both in the procession and afterward, placed on the platform draped in purple, out of the coffin for the ceremonial kissing of the image as the people filed past. The faces veiled in remorse. The fear-shortened steps of timid feet going toward the Son of God, what's in store for us if even He . . . ? The desire for the nightmare to be over sooner, for Saturday to come, for the resurrection to be Saturday. But it was still the hour of the black robes, of torches. Of the incense burners swung from side to side, vupt! vupt! as far as their chains would reach. Will it be much longer, Mama? His desire to avoid everything grave and profound surely had come from that night: the plans to flee at the first corner, dodge away from the crown of artificial thorns, from the red robe, flee from the Crucified Dead so divine, but still dead! The procession followed a determined route, it was easy to run away from it, he learned later. What remained difficult was to run away from himself. In the secret depths from which sprang this fount of anxiety it was always night, with real thorns pricking his flesh, on! why doesn't morning come? I want it to be morning.

He sat down on the bench green with moss, everything around him quieter and damper now that he had arrived at the very center of the garden. He ran his fingers over the moss and found it as sensitive as if it had grown from his own mouth. He examined his fingernails, then leaned over to remove the shredded spiderweb that had stuck to the hem of his trousers: The trapeze artist (was it at the opening of the circus?) lost his grip on the high trapeze, broke through the net, and fell headlong into the ring. His aunt quickly covered his eyes: Don't look, dear! but between the gloved fingers he saw the body twitching upon the net, which it had carried along in the fall. The contortions grew farther apart until it was immobile, only the insect leg still vibrating. When his aunt carried him out of the circus tent, the foot, its toe pointed, escaped from the shredded net in a last tremor. He looked at his own numb foot, tried to move it. But the numbness had already advanced up to his knee. In solidarity, his left arm went numb immediately afterward, a poor leaden arm, he thought, remembering tenderly when he had learned that alchemy was the transformation of base metals into gold, was lead base? With his right hand, he gathered up the other arm which hung detached. He put it kindly between his knees, it was too late to run away. And where was there to run, when the only way out of the garden seemed to be the steps? Down them would come the hunter in a cap, eternal inhabitant on an eternal garden, only he was mortal. The exception. And if I've arrived here it's because I'm going to die. Already? He glanced horrified to both sides but avoided looking behind him. The dizziness forced him to close his eyes again. He regained his balance trying to hang onto the bench, I don't want to! he screamed. Not yet, my God, wait a little because I'm not ready yet! He became quiet, listening to the footsteps that were calmly coming down the steps. A puff of air more tenuous than a breeze seemed to revive the path. Now it's at my back, he thought and felt the arm reach out in the direction of his shoulder. He heard the hand being lowered with the rustling sound of one who, familiar but nevertheless ceremonious, gives a sign, it's me. The gentle touch. I've got to wake up, he ordered, tensing himself all over, this is just a dream! I've got to wake up, wake up! Wake up, he was repeating. He opened his eyes.

*   *   *

It took him a while to recognize the pillow he was clutching to his chest. He wiped off the warm spittle that ran down his chin and pulled the covers up to his shoulders. What a dream! he murmured opening and closing his left hand, which was prickly, heavy. He stretched his leg out, and when his wife opened the window and asked if he had slept well, he wanted to tell her about the dream of the garden with death coming up from behind: I dreamed I was going to die. But she might make fun of him, wouldn't it be more news if he dreamed the opposite? He turned toward the wall. He didn't want any funny answer, how irritating it was when she exhibited her sense of humor. She liked to laugh at other people's expense, but she got ruffled when other people laughed at hers. He massaged his aching arm and gave a vague response when she asked him which tie he was going to wear, it was a beautiful day. Was it day or night in the garden? He had thought so often about other peoples' dying; he had even been intimately acquainted with the details of some of these deaths. And never once had he imagined that the same thing could happen to him, never. Some day, who knows? Some day far away, too far for one's vision to stretch, he would lose himself in the dust of a remote old age, diluted in forgetfulness. In nothingness. And now, he wasn't even fifty. He examined his arm, his fingers. He got up weakly and put on his robe, wasn't it strange? The fact that he hadn't thought of running away from the garden. Turning to the window he stretched his hand toward the sun. I did think of it, of course, but the unscrewed leg and the arm were warning me that I couldn't escape because all the paths led to the steps, there was nothing to do except stay there on the bench, waiting to be called from behind, with implacable delicacy. Well then? his wife asked. He jumped. Well, then what? She was smoothing cream onto her face, inspecting his reflection in the mirror, wasn't he going to do his exercises? Not today, he said, massaging the back of his neck. I've had my fill of exercises. Have you had your fill of baths too? she asked as she continued slapping herself lightly on the chin. He put on his slippers; if he weren't so tired, he could hate her. How off key she was!

(She was singing now.) She'd never had a good ear, her voice wasn't actually so bad, but if you don't have a good ear . . . He stopped in the middle of the room; the insect crawling out of the statue's ear, wasn't that a sign? Only the insect moving in the still garden. The insect and death. He picked up his pack of cigarettes but put it down again. Today he would smoke less. Was this pain in his rib cage real or a memory from the dream? He stretched his arms.

I had a dream, he said walking up behind his wife and touching her on the shoulder. She affected curiosity in the slight arching of her eyebrows, a dream? and started smearing cream around her eyes, too preoccupied with her own beauty to think about anything unrelated to it. Besides, it's losing its vigor, he muttered as he went into the bathroom. He peered at himself in the mirror: Was he thinner or was this image just a repeated echo from the garden?

He went through his early morning routine with a moved curiosity, attentive to the smallest gestures, those he always repeated automatically and which he now analysed, fragmenting them in slow-motion, as if it were the first time he had ever turned on a faucet. It could be the last. He turned it off, but what kind of an idea was that? He was saying good-bye just as he arrived. He turned on his electric shaver, looked at it in the mirror, and with a caressing movement brought it to his face; he hadn't realized how much he loved life. This life he spoke of with such sarcasm, such scorn. I think I'm not ready yet, that's what I was trying to say, I'm not prepared. It could be a sudden death, like a heart attack—but isn't that just what I detest? The unexpected, changes in plans. He dried himself with an indulgent irony. That was exactly what they all said. Those who were about to die. And they never so much as thought of preparing themselves, even his very elderly grandfather, almost a hundred years old and alarmed when the priest arrived: But is it time? Already?

He drank his coffee in small sips, how delicious the first cup of the day was. The butter melting on the toasted bread. The scent of the apples mingled with another perfume, where was it coming from? Jasmine? The small

pleasures. He lowered his eyes to the table set for break-
fast: the small objects. Upon handing him the newspaper,
his wife reminded him that they had two social commitments for that evening, a cocktail party and a dinner, shall
we go from one to the other? she suggested. Yes, fine, he
said. Wasn't that what they'd been doing for years and
years, without interruption? The brilliant mundane thread
unwinding infinitely, day after day, yes, we'll go from one
to the other, he repeated. And he pushed the newspaper
aside; more important now than all the newspapers in the
world was this ray of sun coming in the window and
shining through the honey-colored grapes in their dish. He
picked one, thinking that if there were a bee in the garden,
just one bee, there would be some hope. He looked at his
wife spreading orange marmalade on her toast, a yellow-
gold drop running onto her finger and she laughing as she
licked it off, how long ago had their love died? There had
remained this game. This resigned playacting already in
decadence for lack of appetite, laziness. He reached over
to stroke her head, a pity, he said. She turned around,
what's a pity? He gazed lingeringly at her curled hair, like
that of the statue. A pity, that insect, he said. And the leg
going metallic in the final metamorphosis, never mind,
I'm delirious. He served himself more coffee. But he
shuddered when she asked if by chance he wasn't late.

Today he'd go a bit later, he wanted to smoke a last
cigarette, had he said *last*? He kissed his son in his blue
uniform, busy arranging his school bag, exactly as he had
done the day before. As if he didn't know that that very
morning (or night?) his father had looked death in the
eyes. A little more, and I'll be face to face with it, he
whispered secretly to the boy, who didn't hear him; he was
talking to the servant. If I don't wake up beforehand, he
said in a loud voice, and his wife leaned out the window to
call to the chauffeur to get the car out. He put on his coat;
he could say whatever he wanted, nobody was interested.
And by chance do I take an interest in what they say or
do? He fondled the dog which came to greet him with a
happiness so full of longing that he was touched; wasn't it

extraordinary? His wife, his son, his employees, they all continued impervious, only the dog sensed the danger with his visionary sense of smell. He lighted a cigarette, watching attentively as the flame burned to the end of the matchstick. Vaguely, from some bedroom in the house, came the voice of a radio announcer giving the weather forecast. When he got up, his wife and son had already left. He stared at the coffee growing cold in the bottom of the cup. The kiss they had given him was so automatic that he didn't even remember having been kissed.

Telephone for you, sir, the servant came to announce. He faced him: For over three years this man had worked there in his home, and he knew almost nothing about him. He bowed his head and made a gesture of refusal and apology. So much hurry in one's domestic relations. Outside the home, a successful industrialist married to a fashionable woman. The other one had been equally ambitious but she had no charm, and charm was necessary to invest in parties, in clothes. To invest in one's body, one has to prepare oneself every day as if one were going to meet a lover, she repeated more than once, look there, I don't let my attention wander, not a sign of a tummy! Her attention wandered in other ways. The sweet inattention of one who has all of life ahead, but don't I? He dropped his cigarette into the cup: not anymore. The dream had interrupted the flow of his life when the garden cut across it. The incredible dream flowing so naturally in spite of the steps worn down from so much use. In spite of the footfalls of the built-in hunter who came stepping over the maliciously fine sand to touch him on the shoulder: Shall we go?

He got into the car, turned the key. His left foot slid to the side, refusing to obey. He repeated the command more forcefully, his foot still resisting. He tried a few more times. Keep calm, don't get upset, he kept repeating as he turned off the key. He closed the window. The silence. The peace. Where was that perfume of moist herbs coming from? His disinterested hands rested on the seat. The landscape came closer in an aura of old copper, was it growing lighter or darker? He lifted his head toward the greenish sky, the moon with its bald head exposed, crowned with leaves. Then he was hesitating on the pathway bordered by dark foliage, but what's this? Am I in the garden, again?!! And awake this time, he realized with alarm, looking at the tie he had chosen for that day. He touched the fig tree, yes, the fig tree again. He proceeded down the path; a little farther, and he would come to the dry fountain. The girl with the corroded feet was still in suspense, undecided, afraid to get her feet wet. Just like him, such care never to commit himself, not to take responsibility for anything except superficially. One candle for God, another for the Devil. He smiled at his own open hands, offering themselves. I spent my life this way, he thought, burying them in my pockets in a desperate impulse to go deeper. He drew away before the furry insect could emerge from inside the small ear, wasn't it absurd? For reality to imitate a dream in this game where memory was subject to a determined plan. Determined by whom? He whistled and the Christ of the procession became outlined in the impenetrable coffin, so high. His mother wrapped him up quickly in the shawl, the Senhor dos Passos uniform was light, and it had gotten cold, are you cold, son? Was everything happening more quickly or was it his impression? The funeral march went faster amidst the torches and chains blowing smoke and cinders. And if I had another chance? he cried. Too late, the Christ was already distant.

The bench in the center of the garden. He removed the torn spiderweb and between his fingers (mossy like the bench) caught a glimpse of the body of the old trapeze artist tangled in the threads of the net, only his leg alive. He gave it a caress, but the leg didn't react. He felt his arm drop, metallic, how did alchemy work? If it weren't for the molten lead that was filling his chest, he would go whirling off down the pathway, I found it! I found it! The happiness was almost unbearable: The first time, I escaped by waking up. This time I'll escape by falling asleep. Wasn't it simple? He rested his head on the back of the car seat, but wasn't it subtle? To trick death this way going out through the door of sleep. I need to sleep, he murmured closing his eyes. Amidst the grayish-green somnolence he saw that he was taking up the dream again at the exact point it had been interrupted. The stairway. The footsteps. He felt his shoulder being touched lightly and turned around.

The X in the Problem

With the television on top of the pile of newspapers, the picture got even worse. Cesar started to shake it, I wish I could find Silésio so I could stick this goddamn thing up his ass, goddamnit, goddamnit! Last night, he'd given the set such a whack that Kojak's face, multiplied by six, was reduced to four, but today he couldn't take risks, the pharmacist had just finished answering the questions about snakes, in a little while it would be Aryosvaldo's turn. Look there at the banners opening, what a beauty of an auditorium, my God, there are so many banners, even flags, everybody's cheering, we're with you, Aryosvaldo! We're behind you!

"And this damn TV! I can't see anything, what's this? Is it him coming on, Clorinda? Is it Ary? That one there, isn't it him?"

"Which one, him there? Eeeh, it's really bad, wait, it looks like the commercial, isn't it a commercial? Do something with the sound, Cesar, I can't hear what it says, I bet water got inside the set, it was on the stove when the flood got worse. And tomorrow it's going to rain more, you know that? The man on the news said. More water, Mother of God, this house is rotting away, just smell it, nobody can stand that stench. Turn the antenna around, Cesar, no, not that way, it's gone! There, it's all messed up, now look, it's acting as if the Devil himself was inside. Shake it!"

"Turn it off and then turn it on again, Dad," said Duda.

Cesar obeyed, pulling the antenna from side to side in a distorted circle, how's that? Any better? He pushed it in, jerked it out hard and suddenly found himself holding the antenna in his hand. He threw it away from him, son-of-a-bitch, today of all days, why today? He pounded himself on the head, kicked the dog, which ran off yelping, and stepped in front of the screen. He knelt humbly and began to turn the knobs again, with the soft motions of a safe-cracker trying to discover the secret combination through his fingertips. The sweat began to run down his lined forehead. The black and white image also was running pastellike, the silhouettes melting like wax in the fire, the liquid evaporating in the composition and decomposition of the images—a magic lesson proving that nothing is lost, everything is transformed within the crackling of the machine, which turned voices and laughter to metal, fragmenting them in small explosions.

"Whenever anything happens this turd gets fucked up, the day of the game, remember? Same thing. Right exactly at the time of the goal, everything disappears, ball, net, it's like there's an eye hidden inside there to know which part a guy wants to see and right then it all disappears. I'll throw this piece of shit into the river yet."

"And it's up higher, you know that, Cesar? The guy on the news said it's going to be just like last Sunday, the sky's black. This wall here won't hold up. What's that noise? The rain?"

"Shut up, Clorinda. Bunch of crap, that guy doesn't know a damn thing. The worst is over. Everything's fine. The social service woman promised to help, she talked to you, didn't she? So, everything's fine, now what I want is that stupid cat to sit up there on top, when he sits there it gets better, where's that cat?"

"Yesterday they had meat over at Mercedes', you'll see, they probably cooked him," said Clorinda, returning her gaze slowly to the ceiling. "Is that rain?"

"Is it a little better? Oh, Christ, I'd be satisfied if I could just hear," sighed Cesar, rubbing his palm over his sweaty face. "Remember that story about the diamond necklace, Duda? The Emperor asked the Marquise to give

back the necklace, right? Wasn't that it, Duda? he asked
for the necklace, didn't he? Answer!''

Duda opened his fly and began to scratch himself.

''The necklace or a crown, I don't remember now.
Mário da Nena said that program is all rigged, everything
is all fixed up beforehand, questions and answers, he
knows Aryosvaldo. Says he's a small-time hairdresser who
knows as much about this Marquise dos Santos as we do.''

''Small-time is him. Stupid pimp, he's just jealous.
Envious. You're going to see today how beautiful Ary is,
shit, the bet will go up to a million. And Ary'll get that
million easy, didn't you see him last time? The other guys
want to trick him, but he doesn't fall for their bait, they're
out of luck . . .''

''Wait, Dad, what's that there? Is it him that came on?''

''What a confused mess, look there, boy, I think that's
him, that one there in white, isn't that him? You have to
guess, goddamn it, isn't it a commercial?''

''A cigarette commercial, I know it by the music, that
thing's a boat, the guy's in a boat, smoking. Circe smokes
that brand, the big cow. Creuza too, everything Circe does
she does too.''

''Almost died from getting beaten up so much,'' said
Clorinda, pulling the dog close to her and her son perched
on the rolled-up mattresses. ''And did it do any good?''

The fool went on the same way, pretty soon she'd be
just like her sister, lost in disease and with a swollen belly
every year, after all the trouble of emptying it out, it
would fill right up again. Just like the river.

''And now? Isn't that him?'' yelled Cesar, turning the
knobs, but wasn't it enough to drive you crazy? Aryosvaldo
giving the answer and this buzzing, if the sound would just
get better, goddamn it, if—

''He got it right, Dad, everybody's clapping. All white,
someday I'm going to have a suit like that.''

''Look how beautiful, the auditorium full of rich dames,
all of 'em cheering like crazy, a damn flood of people and
him without any pride or anything, hang in there, Ary,
hang in there, fella, we're with you!''

''I think his hair is so handsome,'' said Clorinda, grab-

bing a fistful of blackened straw which was escaping from
a hole in the mattress. She patted and plumped at it
absently until finding a bigger hole into which she thrust
the straw. She dried her hand on her skirt and concentrated
her attention:

"Is that rain?"

"He knows this one too, look at the crowd, I heard
something about jewels, he got it right, he got it right!"

"The old woman who came on is his mother, his whole
family came from the north because today's his last day,"
murmured Clorinda, peering under the dish cupboard. She
was thinking about something else. "Is the program going
to end, Duda?"

"End? No way, this program never ends, Aryosvaldo
finishes up, and Saturday a new contestant comes who
knows everything about Pelé. Mário da Nena says it's all
rigged."

"Doesn't he know the answer to this one? Look there!"
yelled Cesar. He ran to pick up the antenna from the
middle of the pool of water, poked it into the hole in the
set, and began the revolving movement again. "Doesn't
he know? Answer, Ary, answer! We're with you, goddamnit!"

Duda's hand went immobile inside his fly.

"Eeeeh, things look bad, there's the samba music playing,
when it starts it's because the person doesn't know the
answer. *There it is! The—X—in—the—prob—lem!*"

"Oh, poor thing, it makes me nervous," moaned Clorinda
peering beneath the cupboard again. "Miserable smell, I
think this mud came from hell."

Cesar stood up.

"Answer, Ary, answer! Go on, talk! But why doesn't
he say anything? Talk, man, talk!"

"I don't think he knows, poor thing."

Duda began to scratch himself harder. His free hand
sought to hug the dog, which slunk away quickly. He sang
loudly:

"*There—it—is! The—X—in—the—problem!*"

"Didn't he answer, Duda? Didn't he?"

"I heard something about jewelry, I think he's talking about a jewel she wore, an earring . . ."

"She sure had a lot of jewelry, this Marquise."

"Answer, answer!" screamed Cesar, giving the set a whack which made the picture disappear and reappear immediately. "So did he get it right?" He jumped backward with closed fists, punching at the air.

"He did! Look there how they're yelling, gorgeous, man, gorgeous, they're carrying him on their shoulders! What a goddamn carnival! We're with ya, Ary, we're with you!"

"That one there who started crying is his wife, poor thing. A crier," murmured Clorinda, drying her eyes on her skirt.

"I knew it," said Cesar, dropping down on the pile of mattresses. He was trembling all over, his eyes damp.

"Didn't I tell you? I knew it," he repeated, laughing softly, a difficult laugh, almost a sob: "A million. Shit, a million."

"Everybody's crying, what a party. Circe has that record. *There—it—is! Tum—dum—de—dum, The—X—in—the—prob—lem!*"

"No holding him back! Look there, up on their shoulders, what a hell of a victory. Oh, Ary, you deserve it! And that shithead still talking, what is it he's saying now, shut up and go grab the winner, man!"

"There's a rat under here, I can see his little eyes."

"A million. And if Ponte Preta wins tomorrow, can you imagine?"

"The flood carried everything off, even poor little Nando, but these miserable pests are still here. And it's even looking at me, the beast," she yelled, beating on the cupboard with a piece of stick. Then she grew quiet, listening.

"What was that? Rain?"

"They say they're going to have a guy talking about Pelé, but who wants Pelé? Pelé's old stuff, I want Zico, Zico, Zico!"

"I'm going to get plastered, shit, I deserve it."

"Is it the rain, Cesar? Is it raining?"

He opened the door. Stuck his hands in his pockets. His profile showed the clear-cut jaw of the victor.

"A little sprinkle, it's nothing, don't get worked up, everything's fine. Tomorrow the sun will be shining like a bitch."

Crescent Moon in Amsterdam

The young couple stopped in front of the garden and stood there without gesture or word, just looking. The night warm, windless. A little blond girl appeared on the pathway of blue-white sand and came running. She stopped a short distance from the foreigners, observing them curiously as she ate the slice of cake she took from her apron pocket.

"Will you give me a piece of that cake?" asked the young woman, holding out her hand. "Give me a piece, okay, little girl?"

"She doesn't understand," he said.

The young woman pointed to her mouth. "Eat, eat! I'm hungry," she insisted, accelerating the mimic in exasperation. "I want to eat!"

"This is Holland, dear. Nobody understands."

The little girl backed away. Then she began to run off the same way she had come. He moved forward to call to the little girl and noted that the narrow pathway forked into two long arms which curved around to join hands, encompassing the small round park.

"Such a tight embrace," he said. "I think this is the garden of love. At home there used to be a statuette with a nude angel leaning toward his semiclothed love, burning with desire in spite of being marble, he even had his arm around her. Their mouths were a millimeter away from a kiss, if he leaned over just a little more . . . Those two mouths used to drive me crazy, half-open, without being able to come together. Without being able to come together.''

"But what language do they speak in Amsterdam?"

"The language of Amsterdam," he said, sticking his fingers in the pockets of his jacket, looking for cigarettes. "We'd have to die and be reborn here to understand what they say."

"I wanted that cake so much, can't you smell it? I wanted that cake, even a little crumb, and I would chew and chew it and the cake would spread all over me, in my hands, my hair, don't you smell it?"

He cleaned his fingers, dirty with tobacco remnants from his pockets, on his pants.

"Let's sleep here. But see if you can quit crying, do you want a cop to come?"

"I want to cry."

"So cry then."

Limp, she leaned against a tree and encircled it with her arms. Her hair fell over her face in abandon, but through hair and leaves she could see the sky.

"What a thin little moon. Is it a waning moon?"

He advanced to the middle of the promenade and lifted his face, which was bathed in the light of the starry sky.

"I think it's a waxing moon, it's in the form of a C. Come on, dear, there's a bench there."

"Don't call me dear anymore."

"All right, I won't."

"We aren't dears anymore, we aren't anything."

"Okay. Now come on."

"The bench is cold, I want my bed, I want my bed," she sobbed, the sobs weakly subsiding to a moan. "I'm so hungry. So hungry."

"Tomorrow we'll . . ."

"I want to eat today!" she ordered, straightening her body. She turned a hard face to him. "If you really loved me, you'd make a stew for me with your heart and liver, right now. My dogs used to like beef hearts, they were enormous. Aren't you going to make me a stew from your heart, aren't you?"

"My heart is made of styrofoam, and you can't make

stew out of that. I read once—" he added. He pulled her gently. "Come on, Ana, there's a bench over there."

"My heart is real."

"Yours? Styrofoam or acrylic, in the story I read the man thought there was so much suffering all around him, just so much, that he couldn't stand it. He substituted his real heart for an acrylic one, I think it was acrylic."

"And then what?"

He looked at her blackened feet forcing the straps of her broken sandals, then raised his eyes to her raveled jeans, heavy with dust.

"And then, nothing. It didn't work, he had to be born again as something else."

"You used to know better stories."

Beneath the transparent cotton T-shirt her small nipples seemed cold. And it wasn't cold. They had gotten darker during the trip, he thought. Which Ana was the real one, this one or the other? The one who swore to love him on dry land, at sea, in burning heat, in snow, under the bridge, in a bed of gold?

"You lied, Ana."

"When? When did I lie?"

He looked away, uninterested.

"Come on, tomorrow we're going to see the Rembrandt museum, remember? You said it was what you most wanted to see in the whole world."

"I hate Rembrandt."

"Don't rub your face that way, Ana. You're going to hurt yourself."

"I want to hurt myself."

"So hurt yourself. But come on."

"My fingernails used to be clean. And now look at this crust," she moaned, bending her fingers clawlike to examine her nails. She dabbed at the drop of blood which trickled from the scratch on her chin. "Admit it, you want to continue the trip alone, you want to dump me."

Not even that. He didn't want anything, he just wanted to eat. But even that desire was without the old impetus of the beginning. He would also have liked to go dancing off to light music, himself light and dancing between the trees until disintegrating in a pirouette.

"You said you'd be the happiest girl in the world when you arrived in Amsterdam with me."

"I hate Amsterdam. I used to smell so good, I was so clean. I dirtied myself with you."

"We dirtied each other when the love ended. Now come on, let's sleep on that bench. Come on, Ana."

She pulled his beard.

"When did I get so filthy like this, tell me!"

"I already did, when you stopped loving me."

"But you too—" she socked him weakly on the chest. "Do you deny that you too—"

"Yes, both of us. The fall of the angels, isn't there a book? Oh, what a difference it makes. Come on."

"The bench is cold."

When he took her by the waist, he was actually somewhat startled: It was as if he were carrying a child, exactly that little girl who had fled a little while ago with her piece of cake. He wanted to be touched. And he discovered that he was more disturbed by the fright of the little girl than by the body he was now carrying as one carries a dusty store mannequin, without knowing what to do with it. He deposited it on the bench and sat down to one side. Nevertheless, it was a crescent moon. And they were in Amsterdam. He opened his arms. So hollow. Light. He could go flying off through the garden, through the city. Only his heart had weight, wasn't it strange? Where did this weight come from? From the memories? Remembering love was worse than the absence of it.

"And where are the others? For the trip? Didn't you say that here was their kingdom?" she asked, bending her body forward until her chin touched her knees. "All invention, this business of Mars being rocky desert. I went there once, I'd like so much to go back. I detest this garden."

"We lost the other one."

"What other one?"

Her voice had changed too; it was as if it were coming from the bottom of a chilly cavern. Without an exit. If at least he could communicate to her this feeling of distance between them. Neither pity nor rancor.

"Did you know, Ana? Certain stars are as light as air, one could carry them in a suitcase. A bag full of stars. Can you imagine the fright of the man who tried to steal the bag? His hands would sparkle forever, so bright he wouldn't be able to take off his gloves."

"Look at my fingernails. Even the little girl ran away from me," she complained, hugging her legs.

"She suspected you were going to grab her cake."

"Look at my fingernails. Do you suppose here too they give food in exchange for blood?"

"I don't know."

"Horrible food. That food in Morocco," she said scuffing the sole of her sandal in the sand.

"Our blood is probably horrible blood, too."

The silence slowly formed itself out of the small noises of plants and animals until it wove a tenuous web, which passed by the foliage imponderable, got caught on a leaf, and proceeded rippling until it tore itself on the beak of a bird.

"I want some hot chocolate with cake. Or cream, I'd get a spoonful of cream and smear it all over my mouth, I'd open my mouth . . ."

She opened her mouth, closed her eyes.

He smiled. "I'm hearing music, we could dance. If we loved each other, we'd go dancing off."

She lifted her hand and touched her fingertips to her hair, her mouth.

"Now what? What happens when there's no more love left?"

He almost put his hand into his pocket to get a cigarette again, where had he smoked the last one?

"Blow into the wind, and we'll turn into something else."

"Like what?"

"I don't know. I don't want to be a person again, I'd have to live together with other people and other people—" he murmured. "I'd like to be a little bird, one day I saw a little bird with blue feathers and shiny eyes. I think I'd like to be that bird."

"You'd never have me for a companion, never. I like honey, I think I want to be a butterfly. Is a butterfly's life easy?"

"It's short."

The wind blew so hard that the little blond girl had to stop because her apron covered her face. She held down the apron, arranged her piece of cake inside the napkin and looked about her. She approached the empty bench. After searching among the trees, she went back to the bench and lengthened her half-disappointed gaze along the promenade, also deserted. She scuffed the soles of her shoes in the fine sand, put the cake away in her pocket, and stooped down to see the blue-feathered bird pecking with disciplined voracity a butterfly which was trying to hide itself under the bench.

Lovelorn Dove
(A Story of Romance)

She met him for the first time when she was crowned princess of the Spring Ball, and as her heart jumped and her eyes filled with water, she thought: I think I'm going to love him forever. When she stepped down, she had a moment of dizziness, quickly dried her sweaty hands on the bodice of her dress (pretending to smooth down a pleat) and, weak-kneed, opened her arms to him, smiling a little sideways to hide the flaw in her left canine tooth, which she promised herself to have fixed by Roni's dentist, Dr. Elcio, that was, if she got promoted to assistant hairdresser. He said only half a dozen words, such as, you should have been the queen because the queen is a piece of shit, if you'll pardon my language. To which she replied that the queen's boyfriend had bought all the votes, unfortunately she didn't have a boyfriend, and it wouldn't help even if she did, her sign was Capricorn and Capricorns had to fight doubly hard to win. I don't believe in that crap, he said, and asked permission to go out for a smoke, they were already dancing the repeat of the *Miosotis Waltz*, and it was horribly hot. She gave permission. But it would have been better not to, she would say later to the queen on the way home, because after he went out, she couldn't manage to lay eyes on him although she looked all over the dance hall, and so thoroughly that the club director came to ask her what she had lost. My boyfriend, she said, laughing, when she got nervous, she would laugh for no reason at all. But is Antenor your boyfriend? marveled the director, holding her tightly as they danced *Nosotros*. Because right after the waltz he left twined around a dark girl in a backless dress, he informed her absentmindedly. A nice guy but one who never kept a job long enough to warm his seat, at the beginning of the year he was a bus driver, last month he was a tire repairman in a garage on Marechal Deodoro Square, but now he was in an auto-parts shop in Guianazes almost at the corner of General Osório Street, he didn't know the number but it was easy to find. It wasn't that easy, she thought as she found him in the back of the garage, polishing a part. He didn't recognize her, what could he do for her? She started laughing, but I'm the princess from São Paulo Chic Club, remember? He remembered shaking his head, impressed, but nobody has this address, man, how did you find it? And took her to the door: The work was piled up, he hardly had time to scratch himself, but he thanked her for the visit, leave her phone, did she have a pencil? No problem, he could remember any number, one of these times he'd give her a ring, OK? He didn't. She went to the Church of the Hanged Martyrs, lighted seven candles for the most afflicted souls and began the Miraculous Novena in praise of Saint Anthony, this after telephoning various times just to hear his voice. On the first Saturday that her horoscope announced a marvelous day for Capricorns, she called again, taking advantage of the absence of the beauty salon's owner, who had gone out to do a bride's hair. This time she spoke, but so softly that he had to yell, speak up, shit, he couldn't hear a thing. Then she was alarmed with his yell and delicately replaced the receiver. She only gained courage with the dose of vermouth that Roni went to get on the corner and then tried again just when there was a car accident in the street and everybody went to look out the window. She said she was the princess from the dance, laughed as she denied having called the other times, and invited him to see a very interesting Brazilian film which was playing right there near his garage, in the São João district. The silence on the other end was so deep that Roni gave her a second dose at once, drink this, dear, you're almost fainting. I think the connection was cut off, she whispered, leaning dizzily against the table. Sit down, love, and let me call for you, he offered, drinking the rest of the vermouth and talking with his mouth almost glued to the phone: This is Roni, the princess' friend from work, you know, she isn't feeling too great and that's why I'm calling for her, nothing serious, thank goodness, but naturally the poor thing is anxious for a reply. In a low, controlled voice (the kind of voice the Mafia leaders in movies have, it really *gets* you, Roni was to say later, rolling his eyes upward) he asked calmly that they please not call the garage anymore because his boss was bitching about it, and furthermore (his voice toughening) he couldn't date anybody, he was committed elsewhere, if I feel like it someday, *I'll call*, got it? Hell, let her wait. She waited. During these days of expectation, she wrote him fourteen letters, nine out of her own romantic inspiration and the rest gleaned from the book *Erotic Correspondence* by Glenda Edwin, which Roni lent her. With recommendations. Because now, love, the thing is sex, if he's Taurus (but what a marvelous voice!) you've got to give it to him right away, Taurians talk a lot about the moon, about boat rides, but what they really like is to screw. She signed them Lovelorn Dove, but when she went to mail the letters, she ripped up the erotic ones and sent only the others. Also during this period she began to knit him a green sweater, double strand (beastly hot but in this city you could never tell) and asked Roni twice to call up disguising his voice, as if he were the announcer of the Intimacy on the Air program, to tell him that at such and such a time, the Lovelorn Dove had dedicated a special Bolero song to him. He's very, very macho, Roni commented with a thoughtful smile after he hung up. And only after much insistence would Roni tell her that he had sputtered with rage and answered that he didn't want to hear any goddamn Bolero, tell her I took a trip, tell her I died! The night the soap opera ended with Dr. Amândio rapturous beside Laurinha, when after so many difficulties true love conquered all, she dried her tears, finished hemming her new dress, and the next day, pleading severe cramps, went out early to catch him as he got off work. It was raining so hard that when she arrived, she was already a mess and with her false eyelashes only on the left eye, the right one had gotten lost in the wet. He pulled her under his umbrella, said he was completely pissed off because Corinthians had lost the soccer game, and asked her between his teeth where her bus stop was. But we could go to a movie, she invited, holding his arm trembling, her tears mingling with the rain. In Conselheiro Crispiniano Street, if she wasn't mistaken, there was a very interesting movie advertised, wouldn't he like to wait out the rain in the theater? At that moment he stuck his foot up to the ankle into a deep puddle and repeated twice, this sonuva-bitching rain! and pushed her toward the bus, which was bursting with people and fumes. Before that, he spoke right into her ear for her to quit pursuing him because he couldn't stand it any longer, he thanked her for the shirt, the key chain, the Easter eggs, and the box of handker-chiefs but he didn't want to go out with her because he was already dating someone else, forget about me for God's sake, for God's sake! At the next corner, she got off the bus, got on another one on the opposite side of the street, went to the Church of the Hanged Martyrs, lit another thirteen candles, and when she got home, took the plaster image of Saint Anthony, removed the little child from his arms, hid it in the dresser drawer, and advised him that until Antenor got in touch with her, she wouldn't let him out or give him back the child. She fell asleep bathed in tears, a woolen sock rolled around her neck on account of her sore throat, the little snapshot of Antenor (stolen from his membership file card at the São Paulo Chic) with a sprig of rue beneath her pillow.

On the day of the Hortensias Dance, she bought a ticket for a gentleman, bribed the ticket man who hung around Guaianazes so he would take the ticket to the garage and asked the owner of the beauty salon to do her hair the way Catherine Deneuve wore it on the latest cover of *Secret Lives*. She spent the night watching the entrance door. The next afternoon, she bought the record *Ave-Maria for Lovers* on sale, wrote on the postcard the sentence that Lucinha says to Mario in the station scene, "I love you more than I

did yesterday and less than I will tomorrow,'' signed it
L.D. and after borrowing some money from Roni, went to
leave at the crossroads near Alzira's the things that Pai
Fuzô had asked her for two weeks ago in order to brighten
and fulfill destinies: a bottle of champagne and a carton of
Minister cigarettes. If she wanted a stronger spell, just ask,
Alzira offered. For example? If she sewed up a frog's
mouth, the guy would start to dry up, lose weight, and
would only stop the day he called her, it was surefire. Just
thinking about doing something so awful made her depressed,
imagine, how could one wish such a horrible thing on the
man one loved so much? The black woman respected her
wishes but recommended that she put new garlic in her
pocket, in the doorway to her room, and save one clove to
stick inside there. Inside *there*? she gasped and stayed to
hear other remedies just out of curiosity because they were
impossible for a girl who was a virgin: How could she get
one of his pubic hairs, intertwine it with hers, and bury
them in a cemetery? On the last day of the year, during a
break that was hardly long enough to gulp down a sandwich, Roni called her to one side, stroked her hair (but
how soft, my dear, was it the oil treatment?), and after
taking her coffee cup out of her hand, told her that Antenor
had set the date for his wedding for the first part of
January. She fainted right there on top of the customer
under the dryer. When she got home, the Portuguese
neighbor lady fixed her an eggnog (the girl is skin and
bones!) and taught her an infallible spell: Did she by
chance have a picture of the beast? Well, she should glue
the photo on a red velvet heart and exactly at noon she
should stick the point of a steel scissors into the ungrateful
fellow's chest and say, So-and-so, So-and-so, what was
his name anyway, Antenor? So, when she stabbed him,
she should say with complete faith, Antenor, Antenor,
Antenor, you shall not eat or sleep until you come and
speak to me! She even took a plate of sweets for Saint
Cosme and Saint Damião, set the plate in the garden that
had the most flowers of those she saw along the way (a
very difficult task because the public gardens had no flowers
and the private ones were closed, with watchdogs), and

went to watch him from a distance as he left the garage.
She didn't see him since (she learned from Gilvan, a taxi
driver and friend of Antenor's who was very nice) on that
afternoon he was getting married, with a private reception
after the ceremony at São Paulo Chic Club. This time, she
didn't cry, she went to the Mappin loan service, bought a
decanter, wrote a card wishing him all the happiness in the
world, asked Gilvan to take him the present, wrote an
enormous L.D. on the tissue paper of the package (she had
forgotten to sign the card), went home, and drank caustic
soda.

  She left the hospital five kilos lighter, supported by
Roni on one side and Gilvan on the other, Gilvan's taxi
full of presents that the beauticians had sent. It's over, she
said to Gilvan in a tiny voice. I don't even think of him
anymore, she added but paid close attention when Roni
told her that now the drifter was parking cars in Via
Pompeia, he thought it was in Tito Street. She wrote him a
note saying that she had almost died but that she regretted
such a foolish gesture that had caused her a burn on her
chin and another on her leg, that she was going to marry
Gilvan who had been very good to her at the time she was
in the hospital and for him to forgive him for all that
happened. It would have been better if she died, at least
then she'd quit hounding me, Antenor said when he got
the note which he ripped into a thousand pieces, this in
front of an acquaintance of Roni's who spread it all over
the São João party at São Paulo Chic. Gilvan, Gilvan, you
were my salvation, she sobbed on her wedding night as
she closed her eyes to remember better that night when she
held Antenor's arm under the umbrella. When she got
pregnant, she sent him a postcard with a picture of Christ
the Redeemer (he now lived in Piraçaba with his wife and
twin daughters) telling him how happy she was in her
modest but clean house, with her color television, her
canary, and her little dog called Frisky. She signed it out
of pure habit; right afterward she crossed out the signature,
but only lightly, leaving under the tenuous network of
scratches *Lovelorn Dove* and a heart pierced by an arrow.
On the day little Gilvan was three years old, with a

handkerchief held to her mouth (she was terribly nauseated with this second pregnancy), she wrote him a letter wishing him all the good luck in the world as a bus driver for a company that ran a line from Piraçaba to São Paulo, and stuck a dried pansy in the letter. At the engagement party of her youngest, Maria Aparecida, she asked a well-known neighborhood gypsy to read her future in the cards just for a joke. The woman shuffled her faded cards, spread them out on the table, and advised that if she went next Sunday to the Interstate bus station, she would see a man arrive who would change her life completely, look there, the King of Clubs with the Queen of Hearts on his left side. He would arrive in a yellow and red bus, she could even see what he was like, his hair graying, sideburns. His name started with A, look there, the Ace of Spades with the first letter of his name. She laughed her crooked laugh (the flaw in her tooth had been fixed, but the habit remained) and said that was all in the past, that she was getting too old to think about such nonsense, but on the next Sunday she left her granddaughter with the child's godmother, dressed up in the turquoise-blue dress she'd worn on her twenty-fifth wedding anniversary, took a glance at her horoscope for the day (it couldn't have been better!), and went.

W M

Soft rain and a steel-colored sky. On Dr. Werebe's desk, the white clock says three o'clock, exactly three o'clock. I got here a little while ago, and the nurse asked me to wait. So, how are things going? he'll ask as he lights his cigarette. How is my sister? I'll ask. The silence helps to open the intricate path here inside, down which I go to the very bottom in order to help her. I too need to descend into hell. And on the third day arise from the dead, I pray a lot but not to the pure saints, I pray to the others, those torn by thorns and demons. I pray mostly to Saint Francis of Assisi with his anguished eyes and wounded hands, he can help my sister, he and Dr. Werebe who accompanies me in this descent, raises me up, and encourages me when I stumble, I became much too involved. How are things going? he asks me as he lights his cigarette. I light mine. And without any hurry, we begin to talk about her.

I go to the glazed door that gives onto the patio. On the hazed-over glass, I trace with my finger a *W* and an *M*, two letters cut out in rain-bright foliage, the rest is mist. My initials and hers, Wanda and Wlado, a family whose names all started with *W*, Mama was called Webe. My sister Wanda. On this *W* she went climbing up, agile with her elastic steps, reached the sharp middle point of the letter, and balanced there at the top, a ballerina in a pink leotard concentrating on her rarest exercise, the satin slippers prolonging the angle. She lost her balance and rolled down the slope of the letter until she stopped crushed at the bottom, in this second vertex that touches the ground. She is still there in the dark, caught between the two walls. Her silence is soft because she is soft. But she doesn't see beyond the wall in front of her. Wanda, my sister, don't you want to put on your beautiful leotard and try to climb up again?

Dr. Werebe doesn't answer. One must wait, he said. I wait. She had a childhood crisis, Mama told me about the months she was obliged to spend at her bedside when she was still a little girl. She recuperated. Learned ballet, languages. Five years older than I and so much better developed, at that time we lived in a luxurious house, Mama was an important and beautiful actress with many men around her. So many servants, but it was Wanda who took care of me, who told me stories. When she decided to teach me to read, she bought a blackboard and a box of colored chalk, in between times I would draw. I learned the letter *M* easily, but I had trouble with the *W*, I remember how she used to laugh when my tongue would twist around the letter. But *W* is nothing more than an upside-down *M*, she explained as she wrote a big *W* followed by an *M*—isn't it simple? I turned a somersault and stood on my hands, like this, Wanda? Is it a letter like this? She grabbed my feet and hugged them to her chest. And taking up the chalk again, she began filling the blackboard with *W*'s and *M*'s all the way to the edge, then wrote on the frame, invaded the wall, went around the window, climbed up the bookcase, the chalk crumbling on the spines of the books, the floor, *WM WM WM WM WM WM WM WM*, isn't it easy? isn't it easy? she kept asking, unable to stop. I got very excited, yelling until Mama came in and shook me furiously, will you please stop this? It was Wanda, I tattled, but she kept on shaking me, will you stop? Mama was a famous actress, and as agitated as a whirlwind. Either she was studying for some role amidst crises of anguish (she was a perfectionist) or she was giving interviews, or trying on clothes, or telephoning, she would take the telephone into the bedroom, lie down, and spend hours talking to some friend or lover. Pills to sleep, pills to wake up, her face always smeared with cold cream. She paid no

attention to either Wanda or me. From behind some piece
of furniture or through the crack in a window, I would see
her come and go, complaining, she used to complain about
people a lot. About the shortness of time which made her
hurry, and when she hurried she kept losing things, where's
my handkerchief, my perfume, my key, my scarf? Get this
child out of here! she screamed once when I got too close.
Wanda consoled me with chocolate ice cream and a story
about Fisherman Martinho, who caught an enchanted flounder, which begged to be let go, it would grant whatever he
wished in exchange. I wish for a house, said the fisherman, who lived in a shack. He went home and found his
wife in a new dress, radiant in the prettiest house in the
neighborhood. This contentment lasted for only one afternoon, because that night she began to complain, instead of
such a common house, her fool of a husband could just as
well have asked for a palace, go back and ask for a palace!
He went, asked for a palace, and when he got home, she
was already muttering, what good was all this gold and
marble if one didn't have power? Return to the fish, she
ordered, I want to be king! Later she began to complain
again, the king's power is so limited, it doesn't extend into
the kingdom of heaven, now I want to be Pope! But one
day she sat down on the papal throne, summoned Fisherman Martinho, and sent him back to the beach again, tell
the flounder that I want to be God. God? asked the flounder. And then everything changed back to the way it had
been before. Although I was a child, in some obscure way
I associated Mama with Martinho's wife, who wouldn't be
content. She would star in a play, and the reviews would
come. The telegrams. The honors. Then she would grow
soft, her wavering smile exactly like that of the goddess in
the print, a plump woman crowned with cherubs in a
gondola drawn by two white swans. Come play with Mama,
she would call from between the plumes of her negligee. I
would go but I was never at ease, watching for the first
sign of impatience: There was always a critic who didn't
comment or another who was slightly ambiguous—but
why didn't last Saturday's audience give a standing ova-
tion? Her suspicion of a conspiracy would grow; she would

point out enemies, discover plots. She would be irritated when the telephone rang constantly or when people accosted her on the street asking for autographs, pictures. But when the time came that the telephone was silent and people didn't go out of their way to see her, she fell into the most complete despair. The vases empty of flowers. People uncaring. The tremor of excitement would last until time for the postman to come, wasn't there a letter today? Neither today nor yesterday, only invitations to exhibits or bank notices, which were torn up with such hatred that I began to pray they wouldn't come anymore. There was still the paper, which she customarily read later, I never understood why she reserved it for last. She always went directly to the arts page, perused the articles, wasn't I mentioned? Who knows, maybe a reference on the next page? Or the next? Oh, what insipidity, what emptiness. She would close the paper with a rustling I could hear even from a distance. Daub on her creams, take her pills, and go to bed. Only to begin everything again when she woke up and, still groggy, would want to know—didn't anyone call? She would pretend relief: wonderful. But her jaw would harden. She avoided Wanda because Wanda had become a young woman, she couldn't stand her. And she avoided me because I looked like my father, that fellow who went out to buy matches one day and never came back. In the bustling excitement of success, she thought it just as well that he disappeared. But as soon as she began to get old, the hate which had been short-lived came back full force. On the opening night of a play she had wanted more than anything else to do (she lost the role to a younger actress), she got into such a state that I took some money out of her purse, ran to the florist's, and sent her an immense bouquet of roses, with a card: to the greatest actress in the world from a fervent admirer.

For a week she nourished herself with those roses. She became peaceful. Dreamy. When she began to twitch again, I sent her a record. And a box of bonbons, and after that another record with the money I kept on taking secretly. I paused when she got impatient, but why doesn't this imbecilic admirer ever appear? You'll see, he's a Negro!

And she ripped up the card. Wanda took care of her, took care of me. And she still found time to mark the linens with our initials, so personal the bath towels with a large *WM* in red, I would wrap up in them to dry myself. When I went to bed, I could feel them, almost invisible in the corner of the pillowcase. Or on the napkins. With curlicues on the tip of a silver pen, losing themselves among the iron arabesques of the front gate. Wanda had a moment of anger when Mama learned it was I who had been pilfering her money, flowers had been getting more expensive. But the very next day—it was my birthday—she left a cake with *WM* written on it in chocolate cream in my room. We sat down around the cake. Dressed up in a long low-cut dress and fluttering as in the old days, Mama offered me a little turtle which we baptized with wine, I christen thee Wamusa! Very elegant in her dusty-rose leotard, Wanda danced for me, for me alone as Mama politely continued to ignore her. Later she clasped about my wrist an identity bracelet with my initials engraved on the silver plaque: *WM*. I kissed the letters, kissed Mama, and put the little turtle in my pocket. My family. A strange family, different from others, but wasn't it that very difference that bound us closer? I slept badly, with a curious feeling that I should be keeping watch. Before daylight I leaped out of bed; on all my books and notebooks, on the covers and the pages inside, the *W*'s and *M*'s multiplied themselves in all sizes and colors. I tried to erase them; the crayon and watercolor, charcoal and India ink were irremovable. I found her in the kitchen, eating a slice of yesterday's cake, with the judicious air of a disciplined girl waiting until time for her German class. She denied it, but ended up confessing in tears that she couldn't resist a sort of command which would possess her, oblige her to mark everything she found until she was exhausted. I dried her tears, don't worry, Wanda, don't worry. I'll say at school that I lost the books, how do you say "forget it" in German?

The hollow days, I've already spoken many times of these days which followed next, when the storm changed its course. The wind stayed in my mother's sails, she seemed less unhappy now that she was writing her memoirs. Busy with classes, Wanda appeared to have set herself to a serious task. The problem of the books was resolved, I assumed the responsibility with the support of a psychologist from school. This relaxation, inward and outward, this calm curiosity for a cloud or a leaf which falls and is innocently and lovingly examined, was this unhappiness? I found it amusing when I came upon the two letters carved with a jackknife on the trunk of the avocado tree, but I shrank back flabbergasted when I went into her room: on the walls, the furniture, on surfaces and undersides of everything, in the mirrors, the *WM* scrawled furiously. Or cut with a knife. I passed my hand over the little leather armchair ripped open from top to bottom, the cotton stuffing escaping from the *W* which gaped wider than the *M*. In the corner of the room, the little turtle was marked down to the livid quick of its shell.

I dashed to Mama's room. She was writing her memoirs but she must have been in a sad part, her gaze was vacant. Wanda, where is she? I asked. Mama squeezed my hand and began to cry, but my dear, Wanda died so long ago! You keep talking about her, going on about her, and it's been such a long time since she died! I stroked her hair, which was now completely gray, when had she stopped dyeing it? Yes, Mama, of course, I won't mention her again, I said. Crossing her arms on the table and resting her head on them, she slept. She had fallen asleep in the middle of a sentence, of a gesture, she'd grown old so quickly. I went out and walked without stopping. Mama and her pills. Wanda and her letters. Did it all begin with that blackboard? But what did it all mean, a desire for affirmation? For ownership? I remembered her long childhood sickness, Mama didn't go into detail but she referred to the fear Wanda had of people and of the dark. Was this fear being transferred onto the initials? Could she be seeking herself in them? So many questions confused me, and I was agitated by a doubt: What if I, through my complicity, was only aggravating her state? I ended the night plunged in a small hell, with a genteel little whore sitting on my knees. She had sweet-almond eyes and perfect teeth, she must have been about eighteen. Narrow shoulders, straight black bangs. Are you Chinese? I asked. Just my mother, she answered, examining the little plaque of my identity chain. She laughed when she saw the letters, but my name starts the same way, want to see? And wetting her finger in the glass, she wrote on the table, Wing. I took her to a hotel. For two days I forgot Wanda, Mama, I forgot that *M* walking upside-down, planted on its hands, I forgot everything in the midst of pleasure; I needed this pleasure made up of amenable pauses, Wing spoke only amenities in her voice softer than a butterfly's wing. On the night of the third day, I bought a package of cherries for her—cherries were in season—left her installed in the small hotel with her record player, and went home. I found Wanda in a rose-colored leotard, practicing. I told her about my poor Chinese love whom I had found in the red-light zone, and she hugged me and whirled me around, so I had fallen in love? She wanted to meet her immediately. Later, I promised, later I'll bring her here. She went to get a bottle of wine to commemorate: If I loved someone, then she did too, because the only thing that could save us (she faced me gravely) was love. Mama had gone to the theater with a friend. We listened to music, drank, and I ended up falling asleep there on the sofa. In the vivid dream I saw Wanda approach me with an evil expression. She came slowly, a ballerina's light step. She bent over. But what was this she was bringing in secret? I turned my face to the wall when the knifepoint drew a *W* and an *M* in the palm of my hand. The cuts were sure, neither shallow nor deep, exactly measured. The cold pain, gushing slowly. When I woke up, the sun was already coming in through the window and burning my mouth. I didn't have the strength to look at my throbbing hand. I tied a handkerchief around it and went to find a psychiatrist for Wanda. Six were indicated to me, one of them Dr. Werebe. She resisted, she had a horror of analysis, sanatoriums. At home with Mama and me at her side it might be bearable, but the day I embark on that sea, she said wringing her hands, I will never come back. I calmed her down, but who said anything about going to a hospital? She would stay with us, living together in our reasonable madness. And I asked her for the razor blade. The knife; she must promise that she wouldn't mark anything else. She kissed the palm of my still-swollen hand and entrusted her identity bracelet to me; a present for my Wing.

At the end of that month Mama died. Her actress friend went to visit her and found her lying in the bathroom, clutching the empty pill bottle. Was it an accident? I asked, and the emergency-ward doctor looked at her more lengthily, she was serene in death, who can say? I bought a bouquet of roses like those she used to receive from the anonymous admirer, and then Wanda, in tears, embraced me: You mean it was you?

We held hands during the wake, talking in low voices about Mama. About ourselves. The night was icy, but Wanda's breath was hot as she told me how good the analysis was for her. I told her how good love was for me. When I went to get the lid to the coffin, I nearly swooned, not again! I closed my eyes; beneath my fingertips, I touched the two letters hurriedly carved in the polished wood. I tried to smooth down the splinters with my nails as I looked at my sister, leaning there in the doorway, spiral silhouette of a ballerina in response. But why, Wanda? I asked her when we got home. You promised not to, why? She didn't get upset; she had marked the casket as she marked our belongings, Mama liked these small signs of possession just as I do. Even in death. Where was the harm?

I hear voices in the waiting room, Dr. Werebe is talking to the nurse. So, how's everything going? he will ask me with his professional kindliness, in the first few moments he becomes professional. How is my sister? I'll ask. I always go back to a few events that to me appear to be the doors of the labyrinth: The afternoon I found Wing with her eyes swollen from crying so much, why were you crying, Wing? She closed the windows, let down the venetian blinds, and embraced me with force, for a long time, come into me, she pleaded. Wing knew I didn't like anything dark between the two of us, it was part of the pleasure to see her eyes growing narrower until they dis-

solved and ran into mine, Wing, the light! She didn't
obey, she who was obedient: Leave it this way, she pleaded.
When I turned on the lamp, she quickly tried to hide her
breasts, her lovely, small breasts horribly tattooed with a
W and an *M* in navy blue on each nipple. I covered her
with my body, Wing my love, why did you let her commit
such a horror, didn't I warn you? She didn't answer. She
fixed an astonished stare on me, but what was I talking
about? What Wanda? Then didn't I remember? We went to
the tattoo man together, he promisd to be discreet, only
two little letters—please, she didn't want to talk about this
subject anymore. I love you, she kept repeating. I love
you. Not all the letters in the world could interfere with
this love. When I arrived home, Wanda was in her armchair, leafing through an old photo album. Could this be
our father? Could he still be alive? she asked. When she
saw that I didn't answer, she closed the album and gazed
inside herself. I took her by her singularly childish hands:
Wanda dear, we can't continue this way, I've been your
accomplice, I kept covering everything up, it's wrong,
wrong! Now even Wing saying she didn't go with you to
the tattoo artist, to protect you, I want you to know that
tomorrow I'm going to talk to Dr. Werebe, and if he
thinks you need more intensive treatment, if he advises a
sanatorium, do you promise you won't resist? That you
won't disobey? She looked at me in the mirror, and her
secret face was a reflection of my own. Then she knelt at
my feet and with the tip of her fingers she wrote a *W* and
an *M* in the dust of my shoes.

I erase the two letters made in the condensed moisture
of the window. Here she won't be maltreated, he said. Nor
you either. Talk only if you feel like it, you understand?
The dense rain makes the clump of trees in the middle of
the patio tremble. I begin to tremble too, why is Dr.
Werebe taking so long? He is good, he gives me his hand
as we descend together toward the resurrection of the
flesh, he helps me when I stumble with my burden in my
arms, Dr. Werebe, it's too heavy for me! I say, and he
holds me, in reality Wanda doesn't weigh more than about
thirty kilos but she turns into iron when we begin the

descent. And we need, she and I, to go down to the
bottom of the bottom. Down where the hotel is, I run
knowing what I'm going to find but even so I continue
running, I mount the steps. I open the door, and the first
thing I see is the record player turned on, the needle
revolving in the silent zone, revolving revolving in the
silence and the overturned chair, I don't know how long
overturned, and the needle in the zone I met Wing in the
zone she sat on my lap and her bangs and her eyes like
sweet almonds my poor Chinese love with narrow shoulders come into me she begged and the warm pleasure I
love you I love you I love you come into me she said and
the certainty that now it was cold in the zone of silence
with the needle. Where are you, Wing, and I screamed
when I saw the newspaper open on the floor and the date
the date with the drop of blood spattered it was from the
day before. I stepped on the hard motionless splatter and
farther up the hand hanging out of the bed with its beautiful silver bracelet I went up along the bloody thread of the
arm passed crouching underneath the bracelet how could
the blood trickle down without soiling it don't forget that
detail without soiling it I went climbing up along the dried
ribbon as Wanda did with her leotard climbing up the letter
until she balanced there at the tip Wing Wing don't open
the door! She will plead, she'll implore you but don't open
it and now this rent in the sheets and this breast torn open
Wanda died so long ago Mama said and she didn't know
that she was invisible because I went around cleaning up
after her wherever she went but if I clean this bloody crust
on Wing's breast there will appear the *WM*, lips blue with
the cold and showing right in the vertex her tiny her
beloved heart.

The Sauna

Eucalyptus—this scent, especially, marked Rose and her world of water-steeped woodland plants, greenish filters, and glass receptacles stagnating on the shelves. This the damp-green perfume I smelled when she leaned out over the windowsill to pose. It had rained, and a warm vapor rose from the garden as the sun came out. This is the first portrait I've ever done, I need to get it right, I warned her, and she shrank back into the window. So I kissed her forehead, come on, relax, don't think about what I told you but rather about this orange you're going to hold, like this, you can talk if you want but don't move, nice and quiet holding the orange. When I sketched the oval of her face, she was so serious that she seemed to be posing for a front-and-profile snapshot with a date. Mugshot Rose, I said, and as she smiled, she moistened her lips with the tip of her tongue. They remained lusterless, her anemic lips. My Anemic Rose, you need to put an end to all these vegetables and eat bloody steaks, you need meat! The best portrait I ever did. But what became of it? Marina asked. She must have it, I answered. What became of both of them is what I'd like to know, wasn't it more than thirty years ago?

"Really a long time."

The white-aproned attendant thought I was referring to the duration of the sauna and wanted to reassure me, I could leave earlier if I wished.

"It's nothing. I was just thinking."

"Is this the first time you've come here, sir?" he asked, taking a white robe from the closet. He put the plastic slippers on top of it. "We have a few artists on our list of clients—most of them have massages. Would you like a massage, sir?"

"Just the sauna."

"They say that in Tokyo, these sauna institutes are run by gorgeous girls who do everything to serve the client. One finds that kind of place here, too, but the Orient is something else. Do you know Tokyo, sir?"

The plush fabric of the robe is warm. Music. And the eucalyptus perfume stronger. I take out my handkerchief and wipe my forehead, loosen my collar. To be pleasant is to give him the Tokyo smile, it's easy to be pleasant. And hard, it's beginning to get quite hard, pleasantry saturates quickly: a pleasant fashionable painter. Not first-rate, but the aspiring middle classes think it's first-rate and buy what I sign. I got rich, didn't I? Shit, wasn't that what I wanted? So, don't complain, everything's fine, what's the problem? I follow the white apron submissively, in places like this I become absolutely submissive. The rubber soles of his shoes stick to the green linoleum of the corridor.

"Are you at your normal weight, sir?"

In hell there must be an extra circle, the circle of the questioners, asking their little questions, your name? your age? massage or shower? fire or noose?—without stopping. Without stopping. Marina used to ask a lot of questions too, but lately she's taken to staring at me. A time to ask and a time to stare, and this stare adds, subtracts, and adds again, she's excellent at arithmetic. The women's movement should take advantage of her to do their accounts. But the big thing there, it seems, is interviews. Questions. During one period she asked so much about Rose, had such a fixation, her curiosity was large enough for both of us. One Sunday she forced me to show her the house, I want to see the house, the garden, the window where she posed for the portrait! Where the house had been, they had built a somber apartment building with narrow balconies and washing hanging from clothes racks. Fine, it used to be there, I said. And though I felt a certain relief (it passed, it passed) I had the half-agonized sensation that something had been taken away from me, what? As if the period of those first aspirations had been preserved in the house, so much energy, plans, as long as the house lived the past would be intact. Industrious Rose making perfumes and frames, all the games yet to be played, my fervor, my thirst for recognition—how old was I, twenty? So many possibilities there waiting, this way? That? The building in front of me was the dust-colored answer, furrowed by dripping water and soiled with spittle. I wanted to get the hell out of there, but Marina detained me (just see if I could be let off that easily!). If it weren't for this mania of yours to keep digging up what should stay buried, look there, dear, wasn't that what you wanted to see? There's no more house, or portrait, or Rose—are you satisfied? She lighted a cigarette, a sign she was disposed to talk. I think what really lasts after a long marriage is one's knowing whether the other wants to talk or be quiet. I lighted up too and waited. You mean Rose sold the house so you could take a trip? A statement in the form of a question, Marina is expert at this type of expression. But I won the trip as a prize, have you forgotten the prize? She hadn't, but she remembered that during one of our first encounters in Paris, when I said I intended to stay longer than the prize would allow, I also said I was going to get some money from a house which was being sold, wasn't that the house? And wasn't that the money Rose was going to send me? A sharp girl, this Marina, when we were married I had no idea how sharp she was. Nor that she had such a memory. I think I talked too much, if I ever get married again I'll only open my mouth to ask for the salt shaker. On the second floor of the building there was a yellow towel drying on the clothesline. And diapers, an enormous quantity of diapers. Or dish towels? Do you think those are dish towels there? I asked pointing to the diapered balcony. She threw her cigarette out the window and looked: diapers. I turned on the car radio; the dashboard lighted up for the voice singing faintly, *"Ne me quitte pas . . . ne me quitte pas . . ."* to hear that phrase sung in such a way made it tender, gave one the desire to stay. To hear it without music? Rose didn't say it, she thought it. I turned off the radio. With this computer memory of yours, I began slowly, with this ponderous archive, I hope that you haven't forgotten that Rose was pregnant when I left, I didn't tell you this detail in Paris, I told you later on, remember now? Yes, of course, and she remembers that we didn't have the money for the abortion, a small hitch, we didn't have money, my dear, I hadn't managed to sell a single painting, Rose had left her job at the pharmacy, there was just the house and garden left, but we can't eat a garden, we can't do an abortion in a garden, can we? I repeated, holding her hard by the wrist, we liked this type of game which could end in a bloody nose. She pulled away, you're hurting me, you brute! I kissed her wrist. Lowered my voice: I wanted to sell my ticket and give her the money for the doctor, but she wouldn't accept it, I already told you this, didn't I? She believed in me, she loved me. She knew how important it was for my career, this chance to take a course in Europe, meet people, make contacts. She insisted on selling the house, which was too big now, her uncle in the sanatorium and me going off with no idea how long I might stay—what good was such a big house? And the pregnancy advanced, and the doctor demanding the money in advance, was there any other choice? I know, an abortion wouldn't have been any problem for you, a little industrialist flitting about the world, today a love so poor as this one must seem ridiculous to Madam Marina. But that's how it was. Nowadays everything is so simple, as a liberating leader you know that your sisters have access to the pill, child-care centers, psychologists, at least that's what they claim in the speeches. But back then, have you forgotten? There wasn't any pill, there wasn't anything. And if she insisted on sending the check after the damned abortion, it was because she wanted me to take advantage of the prize, she had faith in my work as no one else ever did. I emphasized the *no one* with such eloquence, but it was no good, Marina was no longer paying me the slightest attention. She took out her comb, combed her hair. She tried to see my reflection in the little car mirror; she used to work in a pharmacy, didn't she? A homeopathic pharmacy, you told me, that sort of thing. She made good money, she was independent, she even supported her mute uncle, didn't she? And so you appeared and started living with her. You committed the uncle to the asylum because you needed more space to set up your studio. Rose quit her job because you needed someone to frame your pictures, right? Wait, let me finish, naturally you began to be successful, prizes, exhibits, and right exactly at that point there appears the *damned* pregnancy, which would add itself to the expense of the journey. Very logical, sell the house. Which means, she was left without a house, without a job, without a baby, and without you, as you were already leaving. Oh, and I almost forgot, without the old uncle who, in spite of being mute, was good company, at least he could hear. All added up, as the poet says, one concludes that your appearance wasn't a very good deal. But one can't talk in terms of deals, you loved her, and when one loves—she added taking a chocolate bar from the glove compartment. She chewed thoughtfully: Another thing, knowing my sisters as I do, I'd go even further, my dear. Even further. I think that your Rose's dream was to have this baby, she loved you, and a woman in love thinks immediately about a child, it's the first thing one thinks about at twenty, a child. You never married her, I know, I saw your papers, my husband isn't a bigamist. But not being married doesn't mean that she didn't want (she paused to examine a fingernail torn on the glove compartment) this marriage, a batch of children, everything on the up-and-up. However, dear, this wasn't your style, and she knew it perfectly; she only adapted herself so as not to lose you. So as not to lose you. I would be astonished to learn that the idea of the abortion was hers, was it really hers? she asked and looked rapturously up at the sky, what a beautiful afternoon! The bluest blue, shall we go to the country house? I turned my face away, because I felt it darkening with hatred. Now she was satisfied, comforted in the certainty that I would continue to be eaten away by thoughts, poisoned. Alone. It's just that the love affair had already ended, I said calmly as we turned in the gates of the country house. What love affair? she said with the innocence the watchman might have had if he'd overheard me.

"Wouldn't you like some coffee, sir? It's freshly made."

The aproned attendant points toward a black man, also in an apron, who is approaching with a tray. I take off my coat and leave it on a chair, and the attendant comes very solicitously to relieve me of the folded robe with the slippers on top. I have the impression that I've been carrying this robe for hours. Years. I accept the coffee only to discover at the first swallow that I don't want coffee, I want to get in the damn sauna and be done with this—why did I take it into my head anyway? I drain the cup down to the granular black accumulation on the bottom, which thickens on my tongue. Thanking the man, I give back the cup, it was excellent. The eucalyptus perfume comes in tepid waves. I loosen my collar and go toward the large glass receptacle full of blue-green mineral water. But the attendant is attentive; he advances in front of me:

"Only a few swallows, if you don't mind."

I don't mind. I watch the water rise in silent bubbles until it runs into the paper cup. She insists I should feel like an egotist, a self-centered egotist. You need to know yourself, confront the truth about yourself, she repeats over and over in our discussions. She has become full of ideas, little Marina, she's changed a lot—oh, how she's changed. A feminist leader. She and some other delirious women manage a newspaper; they create nuclei. All with their consciousness raised, very interesting. She and her band, their faces washed out like the sages of Zion instructing the little children. Quite clever, the young girls. And Marina outdoing them all, she even decided to clear up my distant past. Liberation. Afterward, they'll go off and kill themselves, go crazy. I wad up the cup. Perfect fools. I aim for the wastebasket but miss. Making speeches with their pompous theories, really now, to assume! Assume what? What Rose needed was a man, like all of them, even the lesbians that go to their graves hung up on their fathers. All right, I failed. I hope she found somebody else, some support, wasn't that what she wanted? What they all want? Homeopathic Rose. Fragile Rose. Her eyes were two eucalyptus leaves—that was how I made them in the portrait. I only discovered they were pretty when I began to paint them. At times, Marina repeats the question, where is that portrait? And more than once (she would adore to catch me contradicting myself), I repeated that I gave the picture to Rose, it must be hanging in her parlor, along with the visitors who come every Saturday to play poker, couples from the same block with enough intimacy to open the refrigerator and gulp down their own can of beer. The smartest of them, who watches the plastic arts program on TV, stares admiringly at the portrait. And he makes his evaluation, which keeps rising as the dollar rises, today this portrait is worth a small fortune, undoubtedly one of his best paintings. Back then he wasn't commercialized yet, beginning his career, right? he asks chewing his matchstick, which he moves nimbly from one corner of his mouth to the other, his wife has already warned him that chewing matchsticks gives one sores but he still has the habit. The other guests listen to him with the same respect they show to the excursion guide in Buenos Aires. Oh, and the house (Marina observing me, smiling), why shouldn't it have the same atmosphere as the original one? The smell of eucalyptus escaping from the jars of cologne in the basement, she thought that perfumes needed to age awhile, like wines. The simple furniture. The great pots of maidenhair plant. The ferns. A carport on the right side of the small garden, there must be a car under the canvas awning, the dentist needs a car. But did she marry a dentist? interrupts Marina, who is no longer smiling. It's my turn to be amused. I don't know, I suppose he's a dentist, there was one she used to go to when we were living together, a friend of the family with a practice in the neighborhood. By chance did I go to him for dental work? Marina wanted to know. To this dentist. No, I went to another one, downtown, I answered, knowing very well what she was trying to get at when she looked at me, her thin lips are thinner lately, which gives her a cold expression. The result of the face-lift, which sharpened her profile, is that it? But how original! So, such a fanatical feminist will not *assume* female old age? She will not admit her fifty years? I would certainly like to see that portrait, she said, returning to her thesis, she's always going around with theses, buried in her own or that of some female intellectual from the nucleus, oh! the loneliness. The loneliness that comes and takes me in its beak and then drops me, I fall with nothing to hang onto, no one. In the beginning she was interested in my work. Later she became more and more distant. All right, I cheated on her ever since Paris, and she found out (betrayal turns love rotten, she told me) but isn't it ridiculous? To want me to tell her the truth every time I sleep with somebody, to come up and say, look, dear, I'm just coming from Carla's apartment, we listened to music, drank, and screwed from three to six. I am being frank, and therefore it wasn't a betrayal, betrayal is something you hide, and I did it openly, you have to accept it and go to bed with me this instant if I want you to—is that how I should act so as not to *pollute* our love? I camouflaged as well as I could (one does so badly); I lied to the saturation point. I lost. But if I had been *truthful*, would the result have been any different? She wants me to analyse myself, focus on myself. To know myself profoundly, without deception, without mystery. If I can manage to do this, she affirms, I will be able to paint as I could in the beginning. But, shit, that's the only thing I do. And what good is it, this business of trying to understand myself? There are days when I feel perfect; others, like a beautiful turd. In neither state can I manage to work. I need to feel neither euphoria nor depression, to be just normal. Mediocre, professional. Then I paint one picture after another. I lost the fervor, Marina, that's it. I lost the desire. Too much technique. Too many buyers, the buyers buy everything, who mentioned a crisis? But it's different, I know. You know too, and you scorn me. I made all the concessions, all the adjustments. I ended up rich. And that's the point I want to make. I don't need your stingy father anymore. Once I did, but not anymore, stay in your corner and jingle your money, I'll jingle my own. *Who wants to marry Miss Cockroach? She*

has a box full of money! my mother would carol, her voice
flutelike, like the voice of the cockroach who found a coin
in the crack in the floor. *My mother was true.* Don't you
want the truth, the whole truth, and nothing but the truth?
Well, my mother existed with her dress of swallows on a
midnight-blue background. It's true also that she was delicate and died young. But my father? A professor? No, he
wasn't a professor, dear, nor was he shot on account of
politics, he was a simple hit man who made a living
torturing prisoners, as long as he tortured nobodies, everything was OK, but he got involved with political prisoners,
insisted on using the method of pulling out teeth and
confessions with pliers, and he ended up getting kidnapped
and beaten into bits, they recognized the body because of a
ring with a small red stone which he wore on his finger.
He got what he deserved, said my sister, the girl with
honey-colored hair parted exactly in the middle, like the
saints, I didn't lie when I said she drowned, I always
thought it beautiful for young girls to die of drowning, like
Ophelia, their hair twining around the sea plants. I exaggerated the description on purpose; a touch of Shakespeare
perks up the daily routine. Drowned. She drowned herself
all right, but it was in the whorehouse down on the
Paraguayan border, she ran off with a karate champion,
and one day they came to tell me in a hushed voice (that
kind of news demands respect) that my sister had been
seen in the house of a mulatto madame called Albina,
Malvina, some such name, installed on the border. She
and her professional colleague had already hit the road
after a knife fight during a carnival dance. But my mother
was true with her night-blue dress and her delicacy—will
my mother do, Marina? Will my mother do? I thought
about asking as I warmed myself at the fireplace, it was
cold in Campos do Jordão. Frequently it's cold there, and
cold stimulates the memory. So I came closer to the fire
until I felt my face burn, why don't you leave me in
peace? I felt like screaming. I warmed the cognac in the
bottom of my glass. But do I really want to be left in
peace?

"Your soap," says the attendant, handing me a small

bar of green soap. "And the key to your locker. Would you come with me, please?"

The eucalyptus-perfumed soap. I stick the key and soap inside the slipper, which slides and almost falls from on top of the rolled-up robe. I pile up the objects I receive like convicts in the movies, on their first day in prison. The nostalgic music (isn't it louder?) also from a movie, I recognize it, it's ancient, we heard this together, didn't we? Eh, Rose? I was working on the portrait, but it was getting late, ten more minutes, and we'll go out, there's a movie on I'd like to see, I invited, and she accepted but didn't move, her elbows resting on the window, her water-green gaze fixed on me. At times I would hide in back of the canvas, but even there behind my wall I felt myself observed. Her cheek was blending into the foliage, it was getting dark fast. I grabbed the tube of green and squeezed it down to the bottom, I wanted everything leaf-green, the window, the dress, I too suffocated in a thick joy, like the paint which only ripened to a different color in the orange which she held very gravely. I love you, Rose, do you hear? I love you! I yelled because the painting was turning out like I wanted it; even before I did all the others, I knew this one would be the best. I began to laugh. She held the orange with the responsible air of the Christ Child in the satin cape and golden crown, holding the scepter in his right hand and in his left the starry ball, my mother tacked this picture up at the head of my bed, look here, pray to Him every night so He doesn't let his attention wander and drop the world!

"Do you know the name of that song?" I ask the attendant.

He reaches under the chair for the soap, which has slid off my pile, and gives me back the key which fell with it.

"I believe it's from an old movie. The old songs had a lot more status, don't you think, sir?"

I put the soap away in my pocket.

My hatred for words like *status* and *valid* is almost a physical hatred. Fashionable words. Fashionable people. Later, they wear out and are replaced: I've been hearing less *denotation, connotation*, lately. I'm fashionable too. Or I was.

The spacious metallic dressing room converges toward a white-framed mirror, which takes up the entire back wall. Comfort and order for the clients, who are apparently in order too, I think as I dodge the roly-poly little man who passes by me with Caesarean solemnity in his white bathrobe, his towel draped over his arm like a tunic. I look for my locker number. Of course I can whistle along with the sound track. And even today it's a hit, the film and the music, a love story of the era, Rose was in tears because the bomb went off bull's-eye on the war correspondent who was in love with the Eurasian woman doctor. It's all nonsense, I whispered, and Rose squeezed my arm for me to shut up, this part now was very sad, the girl climbed up the hill where they always used to meet and made a sublime face before the mirage of her lover with the sublime music rising to full volume because love, you see, true love . . . ! Whimpering Rose, I said, giving her a handkerchief, and my hand as we left the cinema, because she was feeling just like the Eurasian girl, about to lose me again. She took me to a vegetarian restaurant, she was vegetarian. But this isn't food! I protested, and she smiled and ordered the salad. Leguminous Rose. She used to season my beefsteak almost without looking at it, once she saw a steer going to the slaughterhouse. She didn't talk much, but she was minute in her description of the suffering stamped in the animal's eye, which rolled wildly as soon as the steer smelled blood. It dug its hooves into the ground, resisted. Finally, worn out, it allowed itself to be led with its head lowered. But I've seen steers too, going along in a line in a narrow corridor, so what? I asked her. I've seen eyes rolling in panic. *That* eye. I didn't want to remember Rose's uncle, the mute. He stared at me intensely that way the night before his hospitalization.

"How hot it is," I say, unbuttoning my shirt.

The attendant gives me a mellifluous smile and offers me a hanger for my coat.

"It's the presauna."

He used to putter with his plants, this mute. When Rose

approached, he straightened his body (he had been kneeling) and showed her a dead root that he had just dug up. She knelt beside him and caressed his thin hair. She cleaned a bit of dried clay that had spattered his grayish beard and wrapped her arms around her knees. She was pallid when she began telling him he should be hospitalized for some treatments, the place was nice, there were trees, flowers. You'll like it, Uncle. He listened and nodded his head yes, he nodded yes. I peeked through the window, and wanted to flee from the scene of the sentimental niece explaining to the old uncle that our house wasn't the ideal place for a mute old man with a mania for plants. I stayed. Between the two of them, there was an instant of immobility and silence, she looking at the ground. He looking at the ground upon which they were both kneeling. Then he closed his fingers around the root, which he was still holding, and root and fingers became all one. He had black fingernails, the soil was almost black. Rose's nails were very clean, but at times there remained traces of the earth that she handled during her experiments. Weak fingernails, weak teeth. And you let her go to a friend in the neighborhood who hadn't even graduated from dental school, marveled Marina. And by this time I don't even know if it really was she or I thinking about this, she asks so many questions I start to mix my own up with hers. Marina, my judge. I keep answering, exactly, Rose was skinny like a branch of that plant that I forget the name of, in our yard there used to be several shelves holding pots of those tremulous little leaves reaching nervously toward the shade. They become more luxuriant when tended by nuns, Rose said, and now I remember: maidenhair. Marina became interested (her interest in Rose is permanent) and wanted to know, why nuns? I don't know, in general nuns are virgins and virgins have powers, the roots recognize the hymenized hands and are grateful, strengthened in the aura of chastity. Mystic Rose didn't have holy images in her house, the plants were her saints. The tuft of violets was Saint Theresa, the thin eucalyptus Saint Francis of Assisi; I've forgotten which saint the purple ipê tree was. Everything within a ritual, an aura, she could see an aura radiate from the plants, brilliant if the plant were healthy. Moribund if it were sickly or dying, just as happens with people, exactly the same. Higher forms of animals and certain people gifted with sight can perceive this aura; Rose thought her uncle was one of them. Marina quickly interrupted me; was this uncle a bit crazy or merely old? I found it simpler not to argue. It becomes terrifying, the pleasure of giving up— gods and peoples, judge me as you will because I couldn't care less about your judgments. Merely old, I replied. He got angry with me, I thought he wanted to kill me, and the asylum was the means I discovered of getting rid of him. The curious thing is that when I give in, Marina loses interest and passes on to another subject. She wanted to know more about the maidenhair plants, by chance did they become debilitated with my arrival? And Rose, wasn't she a virgin? A point which impressed her, that: the fact of a girl over twenty, independent, with some education, and a virgin. I reminded her that at that time, the custom was for girls with no financial means to save themselves, the rich ones could have their little boyfriends and then get married without any problem but Prejudiced Rose was of the petite bourgeoisie. And of the vegetable kingdom, Vegetal Virgins surpass those of other realms, the first time was so hard, Marina, but so hard that I had to go out in the middle of the night and couldn't find a drugstore open. I searched like a crazy man for almost an hour, it was beastly cold. When I came back, she was tranquilly drinking one of her herb teas and offered me a cup. Padlocked Rose, I called her, and she laughed but cried afterward, I couldn't manage to hide my irritation. The poor little thing, Marina said. I stopped to think, why doesn't she act tender toward me? Why doesn't she ever show me sympathy? My mother would have felt sorry for me, not for Rose, she was always on my side. But Marina's not my mother or anyone else's; we didn't have children. Could that be why she became so rigid? But her friends who have children are just the same: aggressive, ironic. You'll see, it's this cretin Movement that's cretinizing all the women. They don't want macho men, but they

turn into macho women. Oh! where are the geisha girls?
The attendant there said in Tokyo. Didn't we always support you? Shit, to get a job is to move out into the street,
to have heart attacks just like us, to swear, is that what you
want? Husbands, children, marriage, all thrown to the
dogs. The important thing now is *the sisters*. Before, our
housemaid could drink kerosene, and Marina at the hairdresser's or at some fairy's style show, the maid is dying,
Marina! And she would tell the chauffeur to send flowers.
Now everything is different, she worries, she takes the
responsibility, questions herself. She went and adopted a
little whore somewhere, who adores being a whore, as
soon as I saw the adoptee I thought, what a sham. But the
nucleus decided they should orient her, educate her, they
say she is the victim of the system— there's another word
at its peak, *system*. They adopted a model who adores
posing nude, if tomorrow she should marry the soybean
king, she'll still pose nude simply because she likes to
show off her ass. OK, fine, she has the right, but what I
don't understand is why she starts complaining later on
that she's a miserably exploited object. What's wrong
with being an object? If it's a useful object, isn't it just
fulfilling its purpose? The case of the cousin, that's one to
make you cry laughing. The cousin was always unhappy
with her rancher husband, no problem, they put up with
each other. After the group orientation, she left him and
now is even worse off, because she went from being
unhappy rich to being unhappy poor. She'll get her balance, Marina says with such assurance it's a pleasure to
hear. She has confidence in everybody except me. If she
sympathizes with the first girl who comes telling her little
story, she sympathized even more with Rose, no posthu-
mous jealousy but tenderness, admiration, I don't know.
That night, for example. My feeling of violation from a
struggle that instead of being pleasurable became a chal-
lenge to resistance, my shame in the drugstore, the things I
asked for at three in the morning so the man wouldn't
suspect, a toothbrush, talcum powder, soap. Ah, and I
almost forgot, do you have plain Vaseline? Then he smiled,

Marina did too, but Marina's smile wasn't very spontaneous, she doesn't find me so funny anymore.

I place my clothes in the cupboard. Put on the slippers. Before dressing in the robe I face the mirror naked. Still in shape, and why not? What about my golf? My tennis, damnit. Maybe just a little bit of belly. I grab the roll with two fingers, here's the excess. I suck in my stomach and turn my profile until I can see my double chin out of the tail of my eye. Do eyes have tails? I asked my mother, and she kissed me, you little silly, you little silly. Rose was a bit like my mother. We were almost the same age, but I felt like a younger brother encircled by her love. I told Marina. It was snowing when we went into the café (Place St.-André des Arts?). Up to the last day, running efficiently about with her black jacket and her nausea, she had started to feel nauseous. But don't tell me she's waiting for you, that you're going back to Brazil next week, Marina interrupted me, and we changed the subject, there was such a hubbub in the café, such warmth. We drained our wineglasses, glug-glug, rubbed our chilled hands, and sniffed the fragrant steam of the sandwiches, how good to be here! How good that you are still free, she said, and never had Rose been so far away, as that moment. True, we had lived together for a few years, but when I went away we were already finished, or almost so. Marina ordered more wine. More sandwiches, oh, what a relief, at last she'd found somebody who was unattached, her last love had been a Swiss fellow with two families, two countries. And now, a man without commitments, a painter! When we met the next day, she asked one or two questions about Rose, but they were fast, casual. I thought they were casual, I wasn't used to her technique. Or she hadn't developed her technique yet, now it's perfected: Even when she is on the surface with the idle movement of a screwdriver uninterested in biting downward, she goes in deep. She complains about my defensive attitude, but don't I have to defend myself? I can't be clear and sharp as she wants me to be, is it possible to express a fact clearly? Things seem so petty. So cruel. If I describe a crime by saying that the woman took aim and fired a shot into her lover's heart, if I simply tell the gesture without the ambiguity, without the circumstances forming the labyrinth that twists and turns until it leads to this objective. Very well, I'll try to be direct, when I met Rose, she was engaged to my friend and roommate, I lived in a boardinghouse. He was providential for me, without his help I would have gone back to Goias, yes, ma'am, Old Goias. Goias is far away, isn't it? Very far away. So he paid my share of the room and board, and furnished me with cigarettes, paint. On the day he left for Recife (he came from there and was going to his father's funeral), he asked me to go and tell his fiancée, she was expecting him for dinner. And there wasn't a telephone. I went, I dined on his dinner and ravished his fiancée, *clearly* that was how things happened. There, I become totally unscrupulous when it's told in that tone; moreover, the episode of the uncle seems abominable. This mute uncle who took care of the garden, the house sat in the middle of a garden, and he lived in a shed at the bottom of it, the shed which I transformed into my studio. One day I dreamed about him, this strange mute who conversed with the plants. At times he would even laugh when they said something amusing, he would laugh softly, but he laughed. They understand each other perfectly, Rose told me. He touches them and through his fingers they communicate down to the roots, have you ever noticed how the flowers blossom faster when he's around? Or that they die painlessly when he picks them? Useless to explain to her that the uncle's discreet madness was gaining strength like the roots, in the darkness. So I had to exaggerate, to resort to hyperbole in order to prove that he could become dangerous. Like on that morning when he looked at me while holding one of those garden tools of his, I actually drew back. You had gone out, we two were alone. So I locked myself in the shed until he went away, I stayed inside painting until you got back, obviously he didn't do anything concrete, but I felt the threat, the danger. She shook her head, denying it, she would always deny, Uncle dangerous? Uncle!!? An old man as inoffensive as the ferns, the begonias, what threat could there be in a rosebush? Perhaps he was afraid, that could be, perhaps I made him insecure, intimidated him. So then he would take refuge in his plants. But there are plants there, too, dear, I said. At this sanatorium I've been looking into, I've already taken care of everything, he's going to be happy in the company of other old people, an old man needs other old folks around him. A month later I took him. He went without resistance, when it was time to get in the taxi he gave me a long look. I took him by the arm, pulling him gently but firmly. I thought he would fight back, try to pull away. He sat down on the seat and looked straight ahead, his hands hidden between his legs, he was always doing this to warm them. Rose was locked in the bathroom crying, for some time now she had been locking herself in the bathroom to eat clandestine sweets or to cry, she was already getting fat. I came back, and she was still locked inside. I knocked on the door, don't be childish, Rose, he is very happy, come drink some wine, positive aura, didn't you tell me that we determine our own auras? I prepared the sandwiches myself while I went on talking, very animated: The shed would be marvelous after it was reformed, the two of us could paint it all, I would fix up my bed in one corner to be able to work late, sleep late, maybe I could exhibit in September, September was spring, a lucky month, we could give a party right in the studio and then think about that little trip up to the Amazon—so many projects, Rose. Including that course I want to take in Europe, I know it's going to happen!

She listened in silence. Drank in silence, her eyes swollen from so much crying. I went to get her chocolates and caramels, which she ate in hiding, there, eat whatever you want, Sweettooth Rose, Crazy Rose! I woke up late the next day. The table was set, but I didn't find her there. I went to the garden; there she was, kneeling beside the pot of begonias, consoling them. Enough of this, Rose, come on, I need you to put together a frame, I called. She wiped her earth-stained hands on her apron.

I tie the belt of the robe. The spongy, warmish cloth retains the perfume of eucalyptus in its folds. The glass pots so transparent they were luminous. The transparent liqueur. The joy with which she came to tell me about her discovery, it was a green liqueur with a light touch of mint, she brought me a small glassful, try it! Its mere perfume was exciting even before the warmth radiated from mouth to chest, to sex, but it's aphrodisiac, I said. We can get rich with this formula, a monks' liqueur! She laughed, and I saw the sparkle of the liqueur in her eyes.

"I've heard your name mentioned many times, but I've never seen any of your paintings, only in magazines. Are you going to have an exhibit, sir?" I follow the white apron, noting that his feet are enormous but his step is soft.

"Only in Washington."

She didn't get rich with this formula or with the others, she didn't have the slightest practical sense. People around her earning money, becoming known. But not her. She ended up conceding the eau de cologne formula to the Italian woman who baptized it with a new name (Petronius?) and put it on the market everywhere. Rose, why did you do that? I asked, controlling myself so as not to shake Obese Rose (she was almost obese) until her petals fell off. She used to glue the little labels on the reused bottles, the old name written in her small green handwriting: *Rosana*. In honor of her mother who used to teach botany, she had met her husband at a plant-life research center, a rare family, all naturalists. I told Marina (what didn't I tell her?) the story of this mother who lived longer than her expected time because Rose made her drink purple-ipê tea, when Death came to get her, it met the mute uncle guarding the tree, and the tree guarding the sick woman. So then it seems that the mute uncle exchanged a few words with Death, and Death turned around, to return only after ten years. Eloquent silence, I added, but Marina didn't laugh, she was concentrating very hard on her needlepoint rug. Back then she used to do these little things to occupy her hands while her mind reached into the far distances, weaving other patterns. I see that the needle doesn't follow the design methodically; it goes back inexplicably to an arabesque it left behind, runs about there, and suddenly reappears again in the lilac spot at the bottom of the cloth, is the law that of colors? Now Marina wants to know in minute detail what happened that night I came to deliver my friend's message: the dinner prepared for him. Rose waiting. And you get there—and then what? Then I stayed, as was inevitable. It had rained, the house was distant, I arrived dripping wet. She wouldn't let me wear those clothes, but made me put on the uncle's overalls while she dried my pants with an iron. The rain wouldn't stop, and I was feverish, I ended up sleeping on some pillows she arranged in the living room. Before going to bed, she made me take some hot orange-blossom tea. My friend needed to stay longer in Recife than planned; he had small brothers and sisters, an inventory, the whole bit. So I began to visit her every day. And didn't she even *mention* getting married? Marina asked out of habit, she knows perfectly well that I never even considered marriage. But you married me, she retorted with that look I know so well, she is about to make that leap with her needle but I beat her to it, with you it was different, dearie. Only daughter, very rich father. A miser who won't say good morning free of charge, this is an interesting detail, what about hope? Doesn't it all add up to this? She laughed, opening the rug on her lap. I never gave up this hope, never. We're getting a little older, true, but to keep the flame burning just as he has, isn't that the most precious gift? And he won't ever die, purple-ipê tea, Marina, hasn't he heard about it? I ask and see that the needle appears to jest as it proceeds, sinuous, into a zone I cannot reach, oh! Marina. Why do we talk so much nonsense, which begins innocently and then sours? You provoke me. I answer in more or less the same tone. But what if I want to forget? You don't let me. Why don't you let me? What are you trying to get at? She folded the rug, put away her wools. It might have been the smoke (she had lighted a cigarette), but I had the impression that her eyes moistened. I don't think you ever loved anybody except yourself, she said, pressing the palms of her hands against her eyes. I loved you, I wanted to say and didn't have the strength. She knows that if I had met her adventuring in Paris like so many others, I wouldn't have taken her to the embassy and married her. She wore cheap little clothes because it was

interesting to be poor, but I was aware that her father
owned textile factories, I found out about his avarice later.
I loved Rose—I could have said. But she knows also that
if Rose had gotten rich with her formulas, if she had
become that kind of woman you take before you on your
arm like a trophy, I wouldn't have made the trip to Paris
alone. I never loved anyone except myself? But if I don't
love myself? You know I live running away from myself.
Or don't you?

I tighten the robe against my chest where the sweat is
already trickling shamelessly. I get on the scales, the
attendant with big feet gives the orders, and I follow them
obediently, time to get weighed now? Then let's get
weighed. I learn I am three kilos overweight, some of
these three kilos you'll be losing soon, sir, he announces,
and I answer that I'm already losing it, the sauna began
when I came in. He writes down my weight on a card. The
scales Rose bought to control her weight didn't control a
damn thing, how could they prevent her locking herself in
the bathroom with her chocolates, her cakes. Rose! I
would call, and she would turn on the faucet, turn on the
shower but she was really chewing. Or masturbating. Masturbating? Marina said, surprised. Do you think she mas-
turbated? Might as well exhaust the inexhaustable theme,
might as well tell her right off that we didn't even touch
each other anymore, the pregnancy was all due to drunkenness, madness. She was already very fat when it happened, a complete accident. But so inopportune that I had
to tell her, this isn't the ideal time. I hate this word *ideal*,
but it was the only one that occurred to me just then. So
she put on her black jacket and went out, on all occasions
she put on this jacket that I wasn't allowed to see, she
thought it disguised her heaviness. It didn't, oh! Marina,
do I really have to go on? It was on the night of my
vernissage. She fixed me a snack, and afterward I kept
drinking, it was still early. I could hear her in the next
room, working on the frames, she liked to work at night,
with music, nibbling her biscuits. When I took the last
swallow of whiskey and said, I'm off, she appeared in this
same jacket. The black purse: I'm going too. I didn't know

what to say. Because for months we hadn't gone out together, I had my friends, my obligations, nobody asked about her, she was naturally excluded. But she didn't care, she was smart enough to know that having gained so much weight she didn't look good in anything. So she dressed without artifice, I even thought once that she actually tried to look uglier. Did she know about your lover? Marina asked. I turned to face her: But who said I had a lover? Marina stared me down, irritated: But did you or didn't you have a lover? Well then? didn't she suspect? She suspected, I answered, and waited for the detailed questions. She didn't ask them. There she was with her purse and black jacket, I went on. Ready to go along. Then the most foolish detail occurred to me, whether the jacket would look better buttoned or unbuttoned. I felt guilty, why had I let her get so fat? And those frightful clothes. I hugged her. The very next day I would give her money for some dresses. I want you elegant again, eh, Rose? She was clutching the handle of the black purse just as a few years ago (how many?) she had held the orange. I looked at the portrait. I looked at her; both with the same water-green eyes pinned on me. My dear Rose, I said, I'm very happy that you're coming with me, everything I am I owe to you, remember? I don't want you to be Obscure Rose anymore, everyone will be glad to see you, even if I don't sell a miserable canvas, we'll celebrate afterward, dinner, a nightclub, a complete bash! But you're freezing, first take a swallow, let's warm up, drink this whiskey. I opened a can of almonds, which she liked, it's still early, better to get there after everybody's arrived. But don't be so tense, take off your coat, come here, I'll put my arm around you. We sat down on the straw mat, drank out of the same glass, and when she laughed, I kissed her. I tasted a flavor reminiscent of vanilla on her tongue, you've been eating pudding, confess! She denied it and giggled. It was ages since she'd laughed, and I was happy. Laughing Rose, just like old times. I took off her shoes. When I took off her blouse, her nipple drew itself up like the leaves of the little plant that goes to sleep when touched, wasn't she sensitive? *Dorme-maria*, echoed a voice from my child-

hood. I kissed her other breast, and it drew inward too,
Waken, Rose! Her eyes darkened. She opened herself
unresisting. Never had I penetrated her so deeply, never
had I taken her so completely in a pleasure which was
almost painful. As if she guessed (Marina listening, pale)
that it would be our last time. I covered her with the jacket
and left her sleeping. Or pretending to sleep. In the street I
began to run. If I caught a taxi, I could still get there on
time. I went dizzily through the starry night with the moon
on the horizon, and I thought of my mother with her dress
the same color as the night, can you see me, Mother? I
yelled and discovered that in death she became part of the
starry globe which the Christ Child held, I needn't fear
that the globe would fall because she was already part of
it, are you there? I called and felt my blood throbbing the
same color as the night, intense. Free. I arrived drunk but
lucid at the exhibit, the stuffy air came out the door to
meet me. I went in grave and blue, glory is blue, Marina,
blue, blue.

"If you need anything, there's the bell," advises the
attendant opening the opaque glass door.

The vapor suffocates me. I close my eyes, which sting
with tears; it is as if a huge pad of humid gauze were stuck
to my face.

"Is it too strong, sir?" he asks.

The gauze pad dissolves, rarefied, and runs off in sweat.
I inhale the eucalyptus, which swirls in hot puffs from
floor to ceiling. I open my eyes and try to regulate my
cough-racked breathing.

"Wait . . . I'd rather go in little by little. It's all right
now, that's fine . . ."

In the dense fog, I slowly distinguish the wooden benches,
spots disposed in a circle, as in an amphitheater. In the
first row, completely naked, is the man who passed by me
in the dressing room. He is limp and lustrous, regarding
his belly falling in successive rolls down to the lowest roll,
which almost covers his sex, small like a child's but
dark-colored. I sit a good distance away so the fat man
doesn't try to draw me into conversation. But he wants
peace and quiet too, since the energies here are all chan-

neled into sweat. We are motionless, only the sweat runs
swift, forming small pools on the benches. On the floor.
Pools isolated from one another like islands. Uncommuni-
cative vessels. But why did Marina say that? That I never
loved anyone. Didn't I love you, Marina? Not even at
first? The desire to mount you and be mounted, that
torment! The satisfaction that puffed me up when I entered a salon with you, not on account of your beauty
because you weren't beautiful but so elegant. Purebred. So
I would take you by the arm, she's mine, she's mine. You
suffered because of my love affairs, we almost separated
during the Carla episode, you mean to say I didn't love
Carla? Nor Rose either? I soiled myself with her blood,
and you say it wasn't love.

"I could drink three quarts of water. Easily," murmurs
the man, raising his head and looking at the ceiling. He
has the eyes of a fish longing for the sea. "One right after
the other."

His legs are smooth like melting wax, the layers that
made the bathrobe bulge now flowing in a dark trail that
filters into the cracks between the tiles. It's not true that I
was ashamed of her, so refined, so sensitive. So much
deeper than all those brilliant women who surrounded me,
I explained to Marina, it wasn't that I was ashamed to take
her to parties—or was I? I liked to have her at home, with
her hair caught at the nape of her neck, wearing her
laboratory aprons. Private Rose. The attempts I made to
render her less clumsy. Less suburban. And now that I
mention these attempts, did I really make that many? Or
did I find it convenient, her shyness, especially when she
really began to gain weight? I don't know why she got so
fat; I warned her. Chocolates, cookies, she used to snack
all day long. I may be calculating. But nobody is *all*
calculation. Nobody is *all* self-interest. I open my robe.
The drops of sweat cross my chest and run together in little
rivulets which flow down opening a path among the hairs
on my abdomen. I stare at my penis, withered like those
roots the mute uncle was going to dig up, listen, Marina,
you mean I never loved at all? How can you say that? I
suppose I never gave myself over totally, that's true, there

was always a part of myself—greater or smaller?—which
coldly watched the other, possessed part. And as for this
business of loving my neighbor as myself, I never did at
all. Stupid abstraction, make-believe. I always received
much more than I gave, agreed, I'm being honest. I lick
my lips: eucalyptus and salt. I loved my work, I used to
work with such love, remember? If we at least had had
children, Marina. But you couldn't have children, I hope
you don't blame me for that too. And so we're alone,
without desire. Without fervor, meaning, I'm without fervor, because you're so passionate over your little sisters,
your newspaper. Liberation. You'll end up liberating yourself from me. You know, Marina, I used to hope we
would grow old together, sex pacified, no more betrayals,
just a tranquil tenderness, without resentment or bitterness.
With our children, I always thought it was stupid to have
children, who get married right away and leave us behind,
ever-so-discreetly planning a rest home for our old age, the
bastards. Like I did with the uncle. And now I miss them,
these children I never had. I could have had them with
Rose. But the idea terrified me so much, quick Rose, go
get an abortion, run, run! You were right, Marina, she
resisted, she wanted our child. And I forced Carla too, are
you crazy, Carla? An unwed mother—is that what you
want to be? It was. But, Carla, I'm not going to separate
from Marina, if you think you're going to latch onto me
that way . . . Then she asked for a whiskey, we were in a
bar. No, that's not it, she answered. That's not what I
want. And I no longer want this child who might look at
me someday the way you're looking now. Carla. She was
courageous, she should join your movement there. I wipe
my chest where the sweat breaks out hotter, in a hopeless
trickle. Before I even complete the motion, new drops pop
out where the old ones were. I rip off the robe. The
burning vapor blows from the four corners of the sauna as
if from the dragon's mouth, there was always a dragon in
my mother's stories with bad men punished to the end,
burning punishment was obligatory. I close my eyes and
see her coming in her midnight-blue dress, and my mother?
didn't I love my mother either? The tears run and mingle

with the sweat that floods my mouth, I'm crying as I never cried before, and I want to cry more, sweat more, pour everything out in this damn sauna, what about my mother?

"Your time is up," says the functionary, opening the door. He comes up to the fat man. Draws back, coughs. "But if you want, you can stay a few more minutes."

The man gets up with difficulty. He picks up the robe, fallen under the bench, puts it on with a painful movement, and goes out, bent over and dragging his bare feet, the slippers forgotten.

"Enough. That's enough for today."

A cool puff of air comes through the crack in the door. And music. I shrink, cover my face with my hands and lean my elbows on my knees. Now the attendant addresses me. I answer through the crack between my fingers, I'm fine. He thanks me and advises me that he will come to call me when my time is up. He closes the door. I discover myself. The tears are running more slowly now, the going made easier for them by the pathways of sweat. I begin to stare at one single point, Marina says this is the way and Marina knows, to look at a point in front of you (I choose the bell) and silently, without disguises, keep shedding off the layers and layers that have accumulated—the naked hours, was it a book? A film? Letting everything that isn't for real fall away. But am I able to make that selection, *I?* Everything's so intermingled, Marina. And you talk about choosing truth like those people of the Inquisition, I think you lived during those times, you must have been the Chief Inquisitor in a brown cap. And I was the maker of counterfeit coins, burned up in the fire you yourself helped to kindle. Then we met in Paris all these centuries afterward, and I've come to melt myself down here, concentrating on one single point until my tears run out. To be alone with myself, you recommend. But I'm not good company, you know, when I stay quiet that way the inky wave begins to rise inside me, miasmas of memories that have no form, they are so long, I don't distinguish faces, words, but only sticky darkness invading the gaps, the empty spaces. The body without air and with all of the air of space, rolling in abandon with nothing to hang onto, and being caught. The beak, the bird descends, and lifts me up in its beak, and then doesn't even hold onto me, it leaves me without support in such unprotected helplessness, I am dying, isn't this death? I look at the red dot and stay immobile, my wish is to go running out of there, yes, I want to drink, talk with the aproned attendant, I accept the coffee, I accept the party, the music, the whore, lie down with the first whore, dine at the first invitation! And I am quiet. If happiness is in movement, I am motionless, rotten with pain and motionless until the last layer peels off. There in the very center, like in the eye of a hurricane, is a place of respite, calm. I breathe easier, it's passing. The anguish of the agony is passing. To coordinate my breathing until the air can penetrate the obstructed funnel to blow on the still-frightened heart, I am moved by my heart, which palpitates like a little bird, afraid of that other bird which carried me off awhile ago. I stroke it gently, calm yourself. I fold my hands across my abdomen, my mother's gesture. But she wouldn't keep looking at her hands, she would look inside. It wasn't like I told you, Marina, you know it wasn't. You asked me to say it myself, so I'm saying it: She's waiting for me to come to dinner, my fiancée, but I have to go off immediately, he said. My friend. Go and tell her that my father died but be careful how you tell her, she's so sensitive. Never mind, I answered, I'm good at these things. When I crossed the garden, I had already decided, I'm going to install myself here. Even my cold, remember? If she feels sorry for me, a poor unknown painter from Old Goias—even more moving, if she should be touched by my poverty. By my lack of assistance. Maybe if she's the maternal type, she'll want to be my little mother. I accepted the dry clothes. I accepted the tea. Tea Rose, I said, and we laughed at the other Roses which were to come later. It's easy to act a part, Marina, but I want to insist on one point, it wasn't *all* playacting, you like clarity, and nobody is either liquid or solid; we're all pasty. Things are tangled, even the dragon has his positive side, I ask myself right now, without cynicism, wasn't it love? Didn't it end up being love? One never knows at the time. Nor afterward. On the night of the *vernissage*, yes, I playacted. I didn't want her to go with me, I didn't want to show off my girlfriend, fat and frumpy in a black jacket. But she got fat when she felt herself rejected. I'm blocking up: I used to say that I was going out for a hot time with other women and didn't even disguise it, she knew. She knew. When that night came, and she said, I'm going with you, I thought immediately, I'll get you drunk, you're going to drink so much that you won't wake up until the next day. But then in the middle of all this (see what I mean?) came the desire. It wasn't in the program, that pained, sweet lovemaking, the exhibit waiting for me, the stars, and she falling asleep afterward, an accomplice in my flight was Generous Rose, I'm sure she was pretending to be asleep. Completely at my service, Rejected Rose, she left her test tubes to take care of my picture frames, she had talent with wood too. We could never afford a maid, she took care of the house all by herself, the garden. The joy which gripped me at times just thinking that she was waiting for me, without resentment. Her gaze clean, her hands clean. The green receptacles and the perfume. The green soup and my rare steak, it was calm. My Tranquil Rose, I told her softly, if you abandon me, I'll kill myself. And I meant it, and that's why I ask myself if it wasn't love, a calculated love but love—is there such a kind? The pregnancy was the unexpected factor. She didn't keep the portrait because I ended up selling it, I had a high bid and couldn't resist. The night before the trip. I'll do another one, Rose, I promised before I left, I'll do dozens later! No, it isn't in her front parlor with the visitors who come to play poker, I made up the story about the dentist, that is, she did get her teeth fixed but afterward they never saw each other, she hardly went out. A wretch of a dentist who made her suffer, she was always having problems with her teeth, the good dentist was mine. The night before the trip. And then she was going out constantly, there was the abortion. The packing. And she had to find herself a room in an acquaintance's apartment. One afternoon (was it the last?) I came home early, I was to leave that night, there she was, quiet, looking at her plants, standing in the middle of the garden. She didn't see me arrive, and she continued standing there with her arms hanging at her side, her hands open fanlike over the planter—it was a gesture of farewell. She couldn't take them along, and she had gone to tell them, she was saying good-bye to her Saint Theresa, her Saint Francis of Assisi—oh! Marina, how I wanted to cry out when I saw her that way, stop everything, Rose, there won't be any more trip, or abortion, or moving, let's stay! Stay. But what kind of a son of a bitch have you turned into to let something like this happen, I kept repeating to myself as I took her by the hand, shall we go? Her hand was icy. The taxi is waiting, Rose, we're late. She buttoned up the collar of her black jacket, yes, let's go. The taxi was waiting, I was in a hurry, Marina, what about my career? My prize? You waiting for me in Paris, Place St.-André des Arts. Two weeks after I arrived, I received the money order she had promised so as to extend my trip but I didn't get any letter. Not even a note. I wrote to the address that she had given me, and the letter was sent back, no such address. I tried our friends, who were actually only mine, no, nobody had any idea where she might be, she was standoffish, wasn't she? Even after our marriage I renewed my search; longing, remorse, or simple curiosity? I don't know. Lost Rose. Lost. Lost. I tried to redo the portrait, and it came out a miserable imitation: only a girl in a window holding an orange and not Rose holding my world, it was my world she held when I gave her the orange, hold it like this, don't move. It rotted. I tried a second portrait and ended up tearing everything to shreds, I was alone and drunk when I called the Devil, I want to paint like I used to, make me paint like before, and I'll give you my soul! Won't you accept my soul? You mean it's such a trashy soul that even you won't take it? When Marina got home, I told her that I wanted to do the damned portrait, and the Devil didn't even take an interest. He's already got too many souls, she said, he wants to get rid of the ones he has. It rotted, the orange. No, nothing can be done over again, half a century has already disappeared, evaporated, how much time is left? And if I were to try again, Marina? Listen, Marina, if I were to try again? Answer me, Marina, what if I were to start over? If you'd help me, if you'd trust me, I could go back to work in earnest. I'll give all this up, it will be a joy to give up all this vanity, this unrest, to work in silence, just the two of us, we'll stay together and who knows, alone? Faith. Love. Suppose love should return, isn't it possible? Answer, Marina, answer! Hasn't it happened before?

"If you want to call for me, just push the button," says the attendant, opening the door for the new client who enters striding firmly, majestic. "Isn't it a bit too strong? No? If you please, your towel." He waves in my direction, had enough? I put on my slippers and roll myself into my robe. I dry my eyes, my face.

"Enough."

He comes closer, the better to see me. I feel like laughing. I must have melted down completely, the blue blobs of my eyes floating off into the distance, in the current, oh, Marina, you're smiling too, you're right, I've promised these same exact things so many times. So many projects. Fidelity, discipline, and isolation—remember? Truly delirious with intentions, words. There's no future, let's not talk about the future because it doesn't exist. There's only now. Now. I only answer for now.

"So?" asks the attendant as he takes me back.

I smile at his enormous feet and announce to him that I'm a bit worn out, but clean.

Herbarium

Every morning I would take the basket and go off into the depths of the forest, trembling sharply all over when I discovered a rare leaf. I was fearful, but I would risk my hands and feet among thorns, anthills, and animal burrows (snake? armadillo?) looking for the most unusual leaves, the ones he would examine at length; those he chose would go into the album with the black cover. Later, it would become part of the herbarium, there was a herbarium in the house with almost two thousand species of plants. "Have you ever seen an herbarium?" he wanted to know.

Herbarium, he taught me on the very first day he arrived at the farm. I kept repeating the word, *herbarium*, *herbarium*. He also said that to like botany was to like Latin, almost the entire vegetable kingdom had its Latin nomenclature. I detested Latin, but I went running to dig out the brick-colored grammar hidden on the last shelf of the bookcase. I memorized the easiest sentence I could find and at the first opportunity pointed to the leaf-cutting ant climbing up the wall: *Formica bestiola est*. He stared at me. The ant is an insect, I quickly translated. Then he laughed the most delightful laugh of all time. I began laughing too, confused but happy; at least he found something about me amusing.

A vague botanical cousin convalescing from a vague disease. What disease was this that made him stumble, greenish and perspiring, when he went up the steps too quickly or walked about the house too long?

I stopped biting my nails, to the astonishment of my mother, who had already threatened to cut off my allowance or forbid me to attend the little parties at the club in the town. To no avail. "You have to see it to believe it," she said when she saw me rubbing red pepper vigorously over my fingertips. I kept my face noncommittal; the night before, he had warned me that I could grow up to have ugly hands: "Didn't you ever think of that?" I never had before, I never cared about my hands, but the instant he asked me that question, I began to care. What if they should be rejected some day like the defective leaves? Or the commonplace ones. I stopped biting my fingernails, and I stopped lying. Or lied less; more than once he told me of the horror he had of everything that smelled of falsehood, juggling of facts. We were sitting on the veranda. He was sorting through the leaves still heavy with dew when he asked if I had ever heard of persistent leaves. No? He stroked the tender velvet of a mallow rose. His expression grew serene when he crushed the leaf in his fingers and smelled its perfume. Persistent leaves lasted as long as three years, but the decadent ones grew yellow and fell apart at the first puff of wind. Lies were like that, decadent leaves which could seem so brilliant but were short-lived. When the liar looked back, the last thing he saw would be a dry, naked tree. But the truthful would have a leafy, rustling tree full of little birds—and he opened his hands to imitate the flutter of leaves and wings. I closed mine. I closed my mouth, burning now as the touch of my fingernails (longer already) caused me greater temptation and greater punishment. How could I tell him that it was exactly because I found myself so uninteresting that I needed to cover myself with lies, like a shining mantle? That in his presence, more than in the presence of others, I needed to invent and embellish so he would be obliged to linger over me as he was lingering now over the verbena—couldn't he see this simplest of things?

He arrived at the farm with his wide gray flannel trousers and his heavy wool sweater knitted in a braided pattern, it was winter. And it was night. My mother had burned incense (it was Friday) and prepared the Hunchback Room, there was a story in my family about a hunchback who got lost in the forest, and my great-grandfather installed him in that bedroom, which was the warmest in the house, there couldn't be a better place for a lost hunchback or a convalescent cousin.

Convalescing from what? What disease did he have? Aunt Marita, who was cheery and liked to wear makeup, answered laughingly (she always laughed when she talked) that our herb teas and clean air would work miracles. Aunt Clotilde, close-mouthed and reticent, gave her standard answer which served for any type of question: All things in life could be altered except the destiny traced in one's hand, she knew how to read palms. "He'll sleep like a log," whispered Aunt Marita when she asked me to take him his sesame-leaf tea. I found him leaning back in his armchair, a plaid quilt covering his legs. He inhaled the fragrance of the tea. And looked at me: "Do you want to be my assistant?" he asked, blowing at the steam. "I've got insomnia, I'm so out of shape, I need help. Your job will be gathering leaves for my collection, get any kind you want, and I'll select them later. For now you'll have to go alone, I can't move around too much," he said, his humid eyes turning toward the tea-leaf floating in the cup. His hands trembled so much that the cup spilled over into the saucer. It's the cold, I thought. But they continued to tremble the next day, which was sunny. They were yellowish like the skeletons of herbs I picked in the woods and burned in the candle flame. But what's wrong with him? I asked, and my mother answered that even if she knew, she wouldn't tell me, this was during the time when illness was a private subject.

I lied all the time, with or without motive. I would lie mostly to Aunt Marita, who was quite silly. Less to my mother because I was afraid of God, and still less to Aunt Clotilde, who was something of a witch and could see inside people. When an occasion presented itself, I would make up stories along the most unexpected lines, without the slightest idea how to get back where I started. All quite as it occurred to me. But little by little, in relation to him, my lies began to be directed, with a definite objective. It would be simpler, for instance, to say that I had picked the birch leaf near the ravine where the thorn tree was. But I needed to prolong the instant that he stopped to look at me, get his attention before he could put me aside like the uninteresting leaves piled up in the basket. And so I would branch out into dangers, exaggerate difficulties, invent stories to lengthen the lie. Until I was cut off with a rapid blow of a look, not with words, but with a look he would make the green hydra roll up mute, while my face would turn red—the blood of the hydra.

"Now you're going to tell me how it really was," he would say calmly, touching my head. His gaze transparent. Direct. He wanted the truth. And the truth was as uninteresting as a rose leaf, I explained it to him just that way, I find truth as banal as this leaf. He gave me the magnifying glass and opened the leaf in the palm of his hand. "Then look at it up close." I didn't look at the leaf, what did I care about the leaf? but rather at his skin, slightly damp, white as paper with its mysterious intricacy of lines, exploding here and there into stars. I followed the ridges and valleys, where was the beginning? Or the end? I paused to view a land of grooves so disciplined that it seemed a plow had passed through them, ah! the desire to lay my head down on this ground. I removed the leaf, I wanted to see only the paths, what does this crossroads mean? I asked, and he pulled my hair, "You too, girl?"

Aunt Clotilde had already revealed the past and present to him through her deck of cards, "And she could reveal more," he added, putting his magnifying glass away in his apron pocket, at times he wore an apron. What did she foresee? Oh, so many things. The only important one was this, that at the end of the week a friend would come to get him, a very pretty girl, she could even see the color of her dress, cut in an old-fashioned style, it was moss green. Her hair was long, with copper highlights, so bright they were in the palm of his hand!

A red ant entered a crack in the tile floor and went off with his bit of leaf, an unmasted sailboat blown by the wind. I blew on him too, the ant is an insect! I screamed, my legs bent, my arms swinging frontward and backward like a monkey's. Hee, hee, hoo, hoo, hee, hee, hoo, hoo, it's an insect! An insect! I repeated, rolling on the floor. He laughed and tried to lift me up, you'll hurt yourself, girl, be careful! Be careful! I fled to the fields, my eyes hallucinating with salt and pepper, salt in my mouth, no, nobody was coming, it was all madness, my aunt was a raving lunatic, she made it all up, pure make-believe, how could it be? Even the color of the dress, moss green? And her hair, she was crazy, as crazy as her sister with her face painted up like a clown's, laughing and weaving her little rugs, hundreds of little rugs all over the house, in the kitchen, in the bathroom, two lunatics! I washed my eyes, blind with pain, washed my mouth heavy with tears, the last shreds of fingernail burning my tongue, no! No, there didn't exist anybody with copper-colored hair who would appear at the end of the week to fetch him, he wouldn't ever go away, *Not ever!* I repeated, and my mother, who had come to call me to lunch, was amused with the demon face I made, I disguised my fears by making fearsome faces. And people's attention would be distracted by these faces, and they wouldn't think about me.

When I entrusted the heart-shaped ivy leaf (a Valentine of trembling veins opening fanlike toward the blue-green edges), he kissed the leaf and held it against his chest. He pinned it to his sweater: "This one will be kept here." But he didn't look at me, not even when I went stumbling over the basket. I ran to the fig tree, an observation post where one could see without being seen. Through the iron grill-work of the bannister, he seemed less pale to me. His skin drier and his hand firmer as it held the magnifying glass over the thorn-bush twig. He was recuperating, wasn't he? I threw my arms around the trunk of the fig tree, and for the first time felt I was embracing God.

On Saturday, I woke early. The sun was struggling against the mist; when it managed to break through, the day would be blue. "Where are you going in that draggy dress?" asked my mother, giving me a cup of coffee-flavored milk. "Why did you undo the hem?" I distracted her attention by telling her I had seen a snake in the yard, black with red stripes, could it be a coral snake? When she ran off with my aunt to see, I grabbed the basket and went into the woods, how to explain to her? That I had let down all the hems of my skirts to hide my skinny, mosquito-bitten legs. Giddy with joy, I began picking leaves, biting into green guavas. I threw stones at trees, frightening little birds who drowsed and dreamed, hurting myself with happiness among the branches. I ran to the ravine. I came upon a butterfly and, taking it by the tips of its wings, put it on the crown of a flower, I release you in the middle of the honey! I cried to it. What will I get in return? When I ran out of breath, I flopped down on my back in the grass. I stayed there, laughing at the misty sky behind the thickly knit boughs. I turned over on my stomach and squeezed between my fingers mushrooms so tender they made my mouth water. I crawled to the small valley of shade behind the rock. There it was cooler and the mushrooms bigger, dripping a viscous liquid from their swollen hats. I saved a little bee from a spider's clutches, allowed a giant termite to snatch the spider and carry it off on its head, kicking, like a bundle of clothes; but I drew back when the hare-lipped beetle appeared. For an instant I saw myself reflected in its multifaceted eyes. It made an about-face and hid in the bottom of the crack. I lifted up the rock; the beetle had disappeared, but in the thin sod I saw a leaf which I had never found before, unique. Solitary. But what sort of a leaf was it? It had the sharp shape of a sickle, the green of its underside spotted with irregular red dots, like drops of blood. A small bloody sickle—was it what the beetle had changed into? I hid the leaf in my pocket, the principal piece in a confused puzzle. This one I wouldn't put with the other leaves, this one had to stay with me, a secret which couldn't be revealed. Nor touched. Aunt Clotilde could foresee destinies, but I could change them like this, like this! and mashed with my foot a grub which was curled up under the almond tree. I walked solemnly back because in my pocket, where before I had carried love, I was now carrying death.

Aunt Marita came out to meet me, more agitated and stuttering worse than usual. Before speaking she began to laugh: "I think we're about to lose our botanist, you know who arrived? The friend, the same girl Clotilde saw in his hand, remember? They're both leaving on the afternoon train, she's as beautiful as can be, Clotilde saw a girl just like her. I'm all goosebumps, look there, I ask myself how Sis can guess something like that!''

I left my shoes, heavy with mud, on the steps. I put the basket aside. Aunt Marita laced her arm about my waist as she tried to remember the name of the new arrival, the name of a flower, now what was it? She paused to wonder at my white face, why are you so white all of a sudden? I answered that I had come back at a run, my mouth was dry, and my heart was beating so loud, didn't she hear it? She laid her ear against my chest and laughed until she shook, when she was my age hadn't she jumped and run all the time herself?

I went up to the window. Through the pane (as powerful as a magnifying glass) I saw them, she seated with the temporary leaf album on her lap. He standing slightly behind the chair, caressing her neck, wearing the same expression he had showed for the chosen leaves, in his fingers the same gentleness with which he had stroked the mallow rose. Her dress wasn't green, but her loose hair had the copper glow which had revealed itself in his hand. When he saw me, he walked calmly out on the porch. But he hesitated when he said that this was our last basket, hadn't they told me? There was an urgent message, they would have to go back this afternoon. He was sorry to lose such a devoted helper but someday, who knows . . . ? We would have to ask Aunt Clotilde in which line of destiny second meetings take place.

I held out the basket to him but instead of taking it he took my wrist: I was hiding something, wasn't I? What was I concealing, what was it? I tried to free myself, wriggling to one side, I'm not hiding anything, let go! He loosed his hold on me but continued standing there, without taking his eyes from me. I shrank when he touched my arm. "And our agreement to tell only the truth? Eh? Did you forget about our agreement?" he asked softly.

I thrust my hand inside my pocket and squeezed the leaf, the sticky dampness of its sharp point, where the dots were concentrated, intact. He was waiting. I wanted then to grab the crocheted tablecloth from the little table, cover my head with it and cut monkeyshines, hee, hee, hoo, hoo! until I could see him laugh through the spaces in the crochet, I wanted to jump off the steps and run zigzag to the ravine, I saw myself throwing the sickle into the water, let it disappear in the current! Slowly I lifted my head. He was still waiting; well, then? In the back of the living room, the girl was also waiting in a mist of gold; the sun had come out. I faced him for the last time, without remorse, do you really want it? I gave him the leaf.

Tigrela

I bumped into Romana by chance, in a café. She was
half drunk but far down at the bottom of her transparent
drunkenness I sensed a thick sediment that stirred up quickly
when she became serious. Then her mouth curved downward, heavy; her expression became fugitive. Twice she
squeezed my hand, I need you, she said. But immediately
afterward she didn't need me anymore, and her fear turned
to indifference, almost scorn, with a certain torpidity thick-
ening her lips. When she laughed, she was an adolescent
again, the best of our class without a doubt. Without a
danger. She had been beautiful and still was, but her
now-corrupted beauty was sad even when she was happy.
She told me she had separated from her fifth husband and
was living with a small tiger in a penthouse.

With a tiger, Romana? She laughed. She'd had a boyfriend who had traveled through Asia, and he had brought
back Tigrela with the baggage, in a little basket. She was
teeny-tiny and had to be raised on a bottle. She had grown
to be just a little bigger than a cat, the kind with tawny fur
and toast-colored stripes, golden eyes. Two-thirds tiger and
one-third woman, she's gotten more and more human
and now— In the beginning it was funny, she imitated me
so much, and I started imitating her, too, and we ended up
getting so involved with each other that I don't remember
if it was she who taught me to look at myself slit-eyed in
the mirror. Or if she learned from me to stretch out on the
floor and rest her head on her arms to listen to music,

she's so harmonious. So clean, said Romana, dropping an
ice cube into the glass. Her fur is this color, she added,
swirling the whiskey. With the tips of her fingers she
gathered up the thin blade of ice that was melting in the
bottom of the glass. She crunched it between her teeth.
The sound made me remember that she used to chew ice
cream. This Tigrela liked whiskey, but she knew how to
drink, she had self-control, only once did she go so far
as to get really smashed. And Romana laughed as she
recalled the animal turning somersaults, rolling across the
furniture until she jumped up onto the chandelier and
perched there, swinging back and forth, Romana said
weakly, imitating the movement of a pendulum. She crashed
down with one half of the chandelier onto the big cushion,
where we danced a tango together, it was atrocious. Afterward she got depressed, and at such times she loses her
temper, she almost leveled the garden, tore up my bathrobe, broke things. In the end she wanted to throw herself
off the parapet of the terrace, just exactly like a person.
Exactly, repeated Romana looking for the watch on my
wrist. She appealed to a man who passed by alongside our
table, the time, the time! When she learned that it was
almost midnight, she lowered her eyes in sober calculation. She remained silent; I waited. When she began talking again, she seemed to me like an excited player hiding
her strategy behind an artificial voice: I had steel railings
attached to the wall, all around, if she wants, she can
climb this railing easily, of course. But I know she'd only
attempt suicide if drunk, and so I can just close the door
that leads to the terrace. She's always so sober, she went
on, lowering her voice; her face darkened. What is it,
Romana? I asked, touching her hand. It was icy. She fixed
her eyes on me astutely. She was thinking of something
else when she told me that at sunset, when the light slanted
over the top of the building, the shadow of the railing was
projected halfway across the living room rug, and if Tigrela
was sleeping on the big cushion, the pattern cast over her
fur by the shadow was beautiful, like a net.

She stirred the ice cube in her glass of whiskey with her
index finger. On this finger she wore a square-cut emerald,

like queens do. But wasn't it extraordinary, really. The limited space of the apartment conditioned the growth of an Asiatic tiger through the magic wisdom of adaptation, she's really nothing more than an overgrown tabby, as though she intuited the need to restrict herself; no bigger than a big cat. I alone realize that she's grown, I'm the only one who notices that she's taking up more space even though she's still the same size, lately there's hardly room for us both, one of us will really have to— She interrupted herself to light a small cigarillo, the flame flickering in her trembling hand. She sleeps with me, but when she's in a huff, she goes to sleep on the big cushion, on her back, stiff as a sphinx.

There must have been so many problems, what about the neighbors? I asked. Romana stiffened the finger that whirled the ice. There aren't any neighbors, one apartment per floor in a very tall building, all white, Mediterranean style, you should see how well Tigrela matches the apartment. I traveled through Persia, you know, don't you? And I brought back fabrics, rugs, she adores this velvet comfort, she's so sensitive to the touch of things, to smells. When she wakes up restless, I light the incense; the perfume calms her. I turn on the record player. And then she stretches herself all over and sleeps, I suspect she sees better with her eyes closed, like dragons do. I had some trouble convincing Aninha that she was merely a well-developed cat, Aninha is the maid. But now everything's fine, the two of them keep a certain distance, but respect each other, the important thing is this respect. She accepted Aninha, who was old and ugly, but she almost attacked the former maid, a young girl. As long as this girl was with me, Tigrela practically didn't come out of the garden, hidden among the foliage, her eyes slits, her fingernails dug into the ground.

Fingernails, I began and forgot what I was going to say next. The emerald slid sideways like an unsupported head and clinked against the glass, the finger too thin for the ring. The sound of the stone hitting the glass roused Romana, momentarily apathetic. She lifted her head and gazed vacantly at the full tables, such noise, eh? I sug-

gested we leave, but instead of the bill she called for
another whiskey, don't worry, I'm used to it, she said and
breathed deeply. She straightened her body. Tigrela liked
jewels and Bach, yes, Bach, especially the *Passion Accord-
ing to St. Matthew*. One night, while I was dressing to go
out to dinner, she came to watch me, she hates it when I
go out but that night she was happy, she approved of my
dress; she prefers classic clothes, and this was a long gown
of straw-colored silk, long sleeves, a low waistline. Do
you like it, Tigrela? I asked, and she came and put her
paws on my lap, licked my chin lightly so as not to spoil
my makeup and began to pull on my amber necklace with
her teeth. Do you want it? I asked, and she growled, polite
but firm. I took off the necklace and put it over her head.
She saw her reflection in the mirror, her eyes moist with
pleasure. Then she licked my hand and went off with
the necklace dangling about her neck, the largest beads
dragging on the floor. When she is calm, her eyes turn a
pale yellow, the color of amber.

Does Aninha sleep in the apartment? I asked, and Romana
gave a start, as if she had just then become conscious of
the fact that Aninha arrived early and left at nightfall,
the two of them slept there alone. I gave her a long look,
and she laughed, I know, you think I'm crazy, but nobody
understands it from the outside, it's complicated. And yet
so simple, you have to get inside to understand. I put on
my jacket, it had gotten cooler. Do you remember, Romana?
Our graduation party, I still have the picture, you bought
some shoes for the dance that were too tight, you ended
up dancing barefoot during the waltz. I saw you whirling
around from far away, your hair loose, your dress light. I
thought it was beautiful, you dancing barefoot like that.
She looked at me attentively but didn't hear a single word
I said. We're vegetarians, I've always been a vegetarian,
you know. I didn't know. Tigrela eats only legumes, fresh
herbs, and milk with honey, meat doesn't come in through
our door because meat gives you bad breath. And ideas,
she said, clutching my hand, I need you. I bent over to
listen, but the waiter's arm reached out to empty the
ashtray, and she became frivolous again, interested in the

cleanliness of the ashtray, had I by any chance tried milk, watercress, and honey beaten up together? The recipe was very simple, you just whipped everything in the blender and then strained it through a sieve, she added, extending a hand, do you have the time, sir? Is there someone you have to meet, something you have to do? I inquired, and she replied no, she had nothing coming up. Absolutely nothing, she repeated, and I had the impression she grew paler as her mouth opened slightly to return to her obscure calculations. With the tip of her tongue she caught the diminished ice cube and chewed it. It hasn't happened yet, but it's going to happen, she said with slight difficulty as the ice burned her tongue. I kept still. A large gulp of whiskey seemed to give her back some warmth. One of these nights when I go home, the porter may come running up to tell me, did madam know? from one of these terraces . . . but then, maybe he won't say anything, and I'll have to take the elevator up, acting very natural so he doesn't notice anything, to gain one more day. Sometimes we meditate, and I don't know the results, I taught her so many things, I learned so many others, she said, beginning a gesture but not finishing it. Had she told me Aninha was the one who trimmed her fingernails? She would offer her a paw without the least resistance, but she didn't let her brush her teeth, she had very sensitive gums. I bought her a natural-bristle toothbrush, you have to brush in a downward direction, very lightly, mint-flavored toothpaste. She didn't use dental floss because she never ate anything fibrous, but if she ever needed it, she knew where to find the dental floss.

I ordered a sandwich, Romana ordered raw carrots, well scrubbed. With salt, she advised, pointing to her empty glass. We didn't speak while the waiter poured the whiskey. When he left, I started laughing, but is it really true, Romana? All this. She didn't answer, she was adding up her memories again, and one of them was leaving her short of air; she breathed deeply, loosening the knot in her scarf. Then I saw the purple bruise on her neck; I looked toward the wall. I could see in the mirror when she retied the knot and sniffed her whiskey. She smiled. Tigrela knew when whiskey wasn't genuine, to this day I can't distinguish them but one night she gave a paw swat to a bottle, and it flew across the room, why did you do that, Tigrela? She didn't answer. I went to look at the pieces of the bottle and saw that it was a brand that had once given me a hallucinating hangover. Can you believe she knows more about my life than Yasbeck? And Yasbeck was more jealous of me than anyone else, he kept a detective watching me. She pretends not to pay any attention but her pupils dilate and spill over, like black ink spreading over her eyes, have I mentioned those eyes? In them I see her emotions, her jealousy. She becomes intractable, she refuses her shawl, her pillow, and goes into the garden which I had specially planted, a miniature jungle. She stays there all day long and through the night, hidden in a thicket in the foliage. I can call her until I drop, but she won't come, her nose moist with dew or tears.

I stared at the ring of water left on the tabletop by the glass. But, Romana, wouldn't it be more humane to send her to the zoo? Let her go back to being an animal, I think it's cruel to impose your own cage on her this way, what if she's happier in the other kind? You've enslaved her. And ended up enslaving yourself, you must have. Aren't you at least going to give her freedom to choose? Impatiently, Romana dipped her carrot into the salt. She licked it. Freedom is comfort, my dear, which Tigrela knows also. She has every comfort, just as Yasbeck had before disposing of me.

And now you want to dispose of her, I said. At one of the tables a man started to sing a snatch of opera at the top of his lungs, but quickly his voice was submerged in laughter. Romana spoke so quickly I had to interrupt, slower, I can't understand you. She reined in her onrush of words, but soon they began galloping ahead again, as if she hadn't much time left. Our most violent fight was because of him, Yasbeck, you know, all that confusion of an old love who suddenly reappears, sometimes he calls, and then we sleep together, she knows perfectly well what's happening, once she heard us talking, when I got back she was awake, waiting for me as still as a statue in front of the door, of course I covered up as well as I could, but she's intelligent, she sniffed at me until she discovered the scent of a man on me, she went wild. I think now I'd like to have a unicorn, you know, one of those blondish horses with a pink horn on its forehead, I saw one in a tapestry, it was so in love with the princess she offered it a mirror to look at itself, waiter, please can you tell me the time? And bring more ice! She went for two days without eating, tigerish, continued Romana. She spoke slowly now, her voice thick, one word after the other with calculated little adjustments in the empty spaces. Two days without eating, dragging her necklace and her arrogance around the house. I wondered, Yasbeck had promised to call, and he didn't, he sent me a note, why is your phone dead? When I went to look, I discovered the cord chewed completely through, the toothmarks all the way up and down the plastic. She didn't say a thing, but I could feel her watching me through those slits of eyes, they can penetrate walls. I think that on that same day she read my thoughts, we began to distrust each other, but even so, do you see? she used to be so full of fervor . . .

Used to be? I asked. She opened her hands on the table and challenged me, Why are you looking at me that way? What else could I do? She must have wakened around eleven, it's the time she always wakes up, she enjoys the night. Instead of milk, I filled her saucer with whiskey and turned off the lights, when she's desperate she sees better in the dark, and today she was desperate, because she overheard my conversation, she thinks I'm with him now. The door to the terrace is open, but then it's stayed open on other nights, and nothing happened. But you never know, she's so unpredictable, she added in a whisper. She wiped the salt from her fingers on a paper napkin. I'll be on my way. I'll go back to the apartment trembling because I never know whether or not the porter's coming to tell me that a young lady has thrown herself off one of the terraces, naked except for an amber necklace.

Dear Editor

"Drought in the Northeast. In the Amazon, floods," read Maria Emilia in the headline of the newspaper fastened with clothespins to the newsstand. She turned her severe gaze away from the young couple on the magazine cover, the girl in the foreground wearing a yellow bikini, the boy behind, hairy arm encircling her bare breasts, squeezing them. Both people were wet, as if they had come together out of the shower. Serious-looking. Why was it these obscene photos all had that aggressive air? Stuck together like animals. And shiny, dripping oily water, ever since Sodom and Gomorrah oils and perfumed unguents had played a part in orgies. Even butter, imagine, innocent butter. The audacity Mariana had to tell about that episode with the butter, the incident she saw in Paris. And shaking with laughter, it was so funny, Mimi, he was dancing the tango with his pants down, so comical! And she confessed she saw the film twice, so as to understand that part better, the idiot. It was the limit. She said there was even a brand of butter that came along and took advantage of the advertising gimmick, useful with or without salt! Three years older than I am, sixty-four and a half. And delighting in the scene of an abnormal man asking for butter. How could the authorities permit such a debauch? Lack of respect. Shamelessness. If a sixty-four-and-a-half-year-old woman let herself be swept along like a leaf in the current, what could one say about the young people? My heavens, the fragile young people, without structure, defenseless, seeing these films. These publications. Television was another hotbed of immorality. Filthy advertisements, an affront. This very day she would write a letter to the *Jornal da Tarde*, a letter spelled out in well-mannered terms. She sighed. There are still well-mannered people, but after all (her expression hardened) even they can get angry. Dear Editor: first and foremost, I wish to introduce myself, a retired teacher, citizen of São Paulo, single. Wait a minute, single no, imagine, why mention one's marital status? That's enough, a teacher from São Paulo who took the liberty of writing to you because no one else comes to mind to whom she can express her revulsion, more than revulsion, her horror in the face of this spectacle which our poor city obliges us to witness from the moment we set foot in the street. Set foot in the street? The thing has already invaded the privacy of our homes, I don't have children, of course, but if I did, I would be desperate by now, this mania of instructing children in sexual matters, these books, these juvenile programs, Dear Editor, and these adult programs that corrupt our innocent children, just like they did with the butter . . . Wait a minute, scratch that part: I'll just say that television is exaggerating, in a general sense, by imposing this bestial image on us, and I'll say that I resisted buying one, I did resist, Dear Editor, but I'm all alone and sometimes the loneliness . . . the dangerous loneliness. But I continue vigilant (she straightened her back, raised her head) so that the same thing won't happen to me that happened to Mariana, such a fine girl, so gifted. A traditional family, descendants of one of the best São Paulo bloodlines, and look at Mariana. "Neat trip. I bought beautiful things but it's time to come home because the charm is wearing thin," she wrote from Manaus. The charm was wearing thin, and her sense of shame along with it. Sixty-four and a half years old. Whoever saw her would think she was a young woman who came to buy some contraband merchandise. Wait, not young, because young women don't worry about charm wearing off, a postcard from an old woman afraid of seeming out of style. And so she tells awful stories, says "hi" to me over the telephone, and wears pants that look glued to her derriere. Before long she'll be wearing T-shirts with things written on the back. She's so afraid, Dear Editor, so afraid. I'm afraid too, it's hard to get old. I recognize that. But what about pride? She squeezed her purse against her chest and looked about her. My hair has turned white, my teeth have darkened, and my hands, Dear Editor, these hands which—it was a running voice—were always the prettiest thing about me. She looked at her hands in gloves. Just as well.

"Would you excuse me, madam?" said the young newsstand man, unfastening from the wire the magazine with the couple dripping water.

She moved back, giving a disapproving glance at the young girl with dark-circled eyes, chewing bubble gum; she wanted the magazine and also a soap-opera story in photographs, "that one there," she pointed and the gum puffed pinkish between her lips until it burst, puf! Maria Emilia quickly turned her disgusted face aside, there you are. I was already composing another letter, My heavens, it wouldn't do to mix one's subjects, *old age* was another topic, now she had to concentrate on this suffocating wave of vulgarity, which was contaminating the very stones. Pollution would have to wait its turn too, the thing to denounce now was this poisoning of the soul. Mariana, for example. She's resisting the air pretty well, she's even healthy in spite of her asthma but what about inside? "Resist, who can? An illusion moaned in every corner . . ." moaned or wept? A time of sentiment. Of poetry. Now the times were marked only by detergents for sinks, deodorants for one's private parts, the number of ads for deodorants! As if simple soap and water didn't work anymore. Mariana heard the propaganda on TV, on the radio, went to the store and bought everything, even homeopathic pills for scant or excess menstrual flow, but, Mariana dear, you had the change of life so long ago! She laughed, my goodness, of course, I get dizzy with all the orders they give, and didn't I end up forgetting? Soon they'll be telling me they've come out with a bionic being for solitary ladies and gentlemen, it was on TV, Mimi, they do anything with you!" Portable. Domestic appliances. Electric shocks.

Sometimes I suspect she's going crazy, that we're all going crazy. That we're gradually being transformed from a peaceful planet into one of total violence and complete affliction (this is a good idea) and therefore, Dear Editor, the population must be warned, the authorities alerted, we must neutralize this perverse influence. You, sir, I—the elite can still be saved. But the rest? When I went to Brasilia by bus, wasn't I taken in like a feebleminded child? Everywhere there was only one ad, Drink Coca-Cola! Drink Coca-Cola! On the highways, in the cities, in the trees and on the store fronts, on walls and posts, even in the restrooms of forgotten cafés in the middle of nowhere, the order: Drink Coca-Cola! And so—poor me! —overcome with heat and exhaustion, and even thinking about ordering a tonic water with lemon or a guarana, I went up to the counter and asked for a cold Coca-Cola. With all the aversion I have for it. I woke up from my stupor drinking that brown stuff that tastes like the soap on trains, there used to be a train (a very long time ago, Dear Editor) with this round black soap hanging on a little chain in the washroom. My father would help me wash my hands, I was a little girl in finger curls, but to this day I can smell the scent of that foam. Imagine if Papa were alive and knew about what happened in the Municipal Theater—a man climbing up on the stage and relieving himself, right there on the gilded moldings, under the eyes of Carlos Gomes and Verdi! Wait, better to cut that part out, more objectivity: to insist only on this, on the danger of this propaganda which, if directed right, can even twist a destiny like that magician twisted silverware. Doesn't the order to drink Coca-Cola correspond, in a way, to the order to make love, make love, make love! One day, instead of seeing the bottle dripping water in the advertisement, I actually saw the mirage of a phallus on the red background. Erect, foaming in the fiery sky, horrible, horrible, I've never seen a phallus but doesn't one really end up making that kind of association? And the saintly, my heavens, how are those who have a vocation for sanctity defending themselves? One would need to have an alligator's hide to withstand such an impact. And this poor skin, so fine in spite of the time, still preserved where it was covered up. Didn't Mariana read in the paper (the fascination she has for these sensational newspapers!) about the case of that young man? Monstrous, the boy that grabbed a Coca-Cola bottle and stuck it almost all the way into the girl? Horrible, by the time they got to the hospital she was in agony, but why did you do this, you monster? the policeman asked, and he answered, screaming, that he didn't know, he didn't know either, he only remembered reading in a magazine once that in Hollywood, during a party that went on for three days, an actor stuck a champagne bottle into his girlfriend when he couldn't manage it himself any longer. But why am I remembering this, what extravagant ideas!

She was startled by the horn of a car, which passed very close to the sidewalk, raising dust, but is it necessary to honk that way? Again she approached the newsstand and skimmed uncertainly over the newspaper flapping in the breeze. And if she were just to read peacefully in the park? But the park must be so dirty, what pleasure could one find in a park like that? That was a good subject for a letter, the dirtiness of our public gardens, the only problem was, it could get too long. And she wanted to be brief. But it's difficult to be brief, Dear Editor. So difficult.

"The Northeast goes through a very dry period which has already destroyed more than 90 percent of its agricultural production, while the Amazon suffers calamitous floods with the arrival of the rainy season," read Maria Emilia. Desperation in scarcity. Desperation in excess. I never had anyone, but Mariana went to extremes: three husbands, not to mention the lovers. Hot blood. If I could have plastic surgery, I'd go right on, but Dr. Braga was final, if you have an operation, you won't get up off the table because your heart can't take it, do you understand? She understood. Thank goodness. Didn't Elza stay on the table? Another victim of advertising, dear Elza. She so regretted Mariana's agitation, prided herself on accepting old age without resistance, the poor dear. But she heard so much about the stars and beauty queens coming from far away to renovate their faces that she ended up being swayed, she was very impressionable. The phone call in the wee hours of the morning, Dona Maria Emilia, I wanted to advise you that Grandma's funeral is to be at nine o'clock, we know you were such good friends. But whose funeral, in heaven's name? Elza's? But did Elza die? No, not Elza! we were together only two days ago, she was splendid! Arrest? Cardiac arrest? Even in the midst of my tears, I could sense the grandson's reticence, I even had the absurd thought, could it be she killed herself? Funeral at nine. When I leaned over the coffin, I understood everything, the dear, the poor dear with her face all painted with Mercurochrome. She died during the anesthesia, when the so-called doctor with the name like an animal, what was his name? Anyway, when he was getting ready to do the first incisions. Imagine, to do a face-lift on an old woman, Elza was at least six years older than I. But is it against the law to get old? Another important point, Dear Editor, there should be a regulation controlling this, all these old people around having operations, their arteries already beginning to harden. Not even the dying escape, remember that cousin of Leal's who had the disease? A month before she died, the poor thing decided to have a face-lift, and the doctor knew, the mercenary. The consolation is that she died looking much younger, that fool Mariana came up and told me during the funeral service.

How about a movie? She looked at the pallid blue sky. Pure. A shame to trade that afternoon for a dark theater, but where to go then? Tea? But was there a decent tearoom left hereabouts? Frowning, she watched the man with plastered-down hair who came up to examine more closely the colored poster fastened to the lower rung of the newsstand. He had brilliantine on his hair, and even without seeing his face she could imagine the cupidity of his mattery eyes (they would be small, oozing yellow matter) glued to the red bikini of the redhead mounted frontward on a chair, the nipples of her firm breasts erect. Boots, cowboy hat, a revolver in each hand. And the bikini so tight between her legs that you could clearly see the mound with flattened hair under the satin, more exposed than if there had been nothing over it. There you are, Dear Editor.

The image of the woman-object, as those girls from the feminist group call it. Intelligent girls, cultured, almost all of them college graduates. But my heavens, if they were just a little more moderate! More discreet. To revindicate so many things at the same time, can't so much change all at once be damaging? Shaking our foundations, I think they are rushing ahead too fast. When I was their age, I never thought, for example, about the word *prostitute*. And one stands up and starts to defend her profession, I thought I wasn't hearing properly, *profession*? And the young thing there in flesh and blood, I had to pinch myself, am I awake? She even had the look of one of these secretaries from American firms, a delicate profile that made me think of an old classmate from Des Oiseaux, Carola, who died before our first communion. I swear I tried hard to understand, to participate in her anger; the trollop was enraged with a series of really deplorable things that the police do to these women. So I tried to enter into her anger and discovered I was actually enraged against her, good grief, what utter nonsense! Couldn't she choose some other activity? To assure her professional liberty, what gall! When the woman lawyer with spectacles stood up, I breathed a sigh of relief; now the level of the discussion will be raised, I thought, and in the beginning she was actually quite good with her historic exposition of the condition of women. I think that expression is so noble, *condition of women*. But all of a sudden she began to talk about the clitoris, why clitoris, and with men all around, I didn't know where to hide my head when she told that in some country or other they make an incision in the woman's clitoris so she doesn't feel the slightest pleasure, sex transformed into a pincushion, a simple instrument for penetration. And she gave other equally horrible examples, I agree, cruelties, all these practices. But to bring it into a debate? I wanted to disguise my horror, show I wasn't shocked, but when I noticed myself, I was applauding after all the rest had stopped, it always happens that through timidity, fear of being center stage, I end up just there. If I frequented that group, I'd end up like Mariana, wearing blue jeans and rings on all my fingers.

The crimes against women, now I remember, that was the theme of the round table. I accuse, I accuse! repeated a girl in a lacy smock, pregnant and defending the right to get an abortion, she had been raped in the middle of the street, and now she was even attacking the Pope, God forgive me for heresy but who knows, in such extreme cases mightn't some measure to interrupt gestation be advisable? I felt very sorry for her, I accuse, I accuse! she repeated with her eyes full of tears, but at the same time, to accept abortion, oh, that's such a strong word. I got depressed, thinking about Mama who didn't have any incision but who never felt the slightest pleasure. And she had eight children. Eight. Forty years of marriage without pleasure—a silent pincushion. But I'm getting off the track, my heavens, how difficult to state exactly what one wishes to say, so many things pop up in the middle. "The Form, cold and thick, is a sepulcher of snow . . . and the weighty Word muffles the light Idea . . ." wrote Olavo Bilac, in *Inania Verba*. My favorite poet, Dear Editor. I always liked poetry. I even used to recite. What if I transcribed these verses at the end of the letter, in the guise of begging pardon? But wait, let's begin at the beginning. Dear Editor: first and foremost I want to introduce myself, a teacher. Citizen of São Paulo, retired. Retired citizen of São Paulo, look there, how silly. A retired teacher, citizen of São Paulo. With two deep wrinkles between my eyebrows from frowning so hard at the girls, I'm not going to write this part, but I remember well the beginning of these wrinkles, wanting to hold back with them the swarm of girls that used to come foaming forth like a river, covering everything, so forceful, one class after another, one after another, why do they make me think of a river without beginning or end? I lost my voice shouting at them to be quiet, my throat grew raw. So then I would frown at them, and they would grow calm, for a few minutes they would be frightened. But soon they would burst forth in wild hilarity again, their little breasts pushing their pinafores, excited, damp, they exploded principally in the summer. I would avoid brushing against them when they came back from recess, the acid smell of sweat and dust stronger, still chewing their banana or bread and butter. The cries, the laughter, the rage—all the same thing. At the end of the year, they would say tearful farewells, give me flowers. They all forgot me. Only I was marked, in this way I have of looking at people, vigilant, distrustful. The truth is, I was afraid of them just as they were of me, but their fear was short-lived. And mine has gone on so long, Dear Editor, so long.

She gave a final glance at the newsstand, where the seller picked his teeth and chatted with the brilliantine man. A haughty lady, far above all this frivolity, the two must have been thinking when she passed in front of them, walking firmly, moved by her own air of distinction. She continued down the sunbathed sidewalk, wasn't it truly delightful, that sun? Her hand went to her coat lapel to confirm it: The camellia was still there. A small extravagance, Dear Editor, today is my birthday, and as it was such a beautiful Sunday, I pinned this flower here. My suit is sober, my hairdo is sober, a sober lady who permitted herself to wear a flower, may I? She allowed her lips to open in a remote smile, which made her think of the Mona Lisa, she had a print fastened to the glass in her bookshelf, the smile just so, reticent, mature in wisdom (she closed her eyes) and inaccessible. She must have been a lonely woman also. Entering old age (she walked more firmly) and intact. She clutched her purse under her arm and crossed her hands limply over her chest, the corners of her shawl swinging and the long fringe hanging as she relaxed her fingers—but what's this? She stopped smiling. That woman there in the miniskirt, walking suggestively beside the man in sunglasses. Varicose veins in her legs. And she unconscious, with the ridiculous little skirt showing off the lace of her panties, where were the police? Aren't there police around anymore? Right behind, a little prostitute (fourteen?) barely balancing on high cork-soled platform sandals, her eyelids heavy with green shadow. Following close behind her, an old man with the profile of a hunter—my heavens, but where's the juvenile delinquency board? In broad daylight.

A strip of blue toilet paper rose from the pile of trash on

the corner and came flying low, undulating in the unexpected wind. She dodged quickly, and the serpentine rolled itself around the ankle of the man who was strolling a little way behind, peeling a tangerine. He went along scattering the rind here and there, a happy sower. Fulfilled. When he came abreast of her, she indicated plainly with a movement of her head the metal wastebasket fastened to a post: "São Paulo is a Clean City" written on the almost-empty basket. But the man went on spitting out the seeds forcefully, like a child in contest with another to see who could spit further. Dear Editor, the municipal government should study with urgency a project for the education of these people, who have the same mental age as those girls I used to inspect as they came out of the rest room: Did you flush the toilet? I would ask. And the faces innocent with surprise: Oh! I forgot. But am I the only one in the midst of this crowd who cares? Who feels upset? She paused uncertainly at the corner. She gazed over the tops of the cars toward the immense movie advertisement on the other side of the street. A Brazilian film? Naturally, if there's a bed, a woman with a raffish expression, and a man in only his underwear, it could only be Brazilian cinema, truly an affront, incredible, how does the censorship permit it? No, the letter wouldn't be about the trash, no good mixing one's topics, the inner dirtiness, Dear Editor, this is worse than atomic waste because it can't be cleaned with a simple scrub brush. She walked faster, there must be another movie theater ahead, she would await the evening in the cinema, thank you very much, my dears, but today I have a date with a group of friends, they are going to offer me tea, you don't mind if we leave it for another day? They protested emphatically, of course they minded very much! Oh, what an ungrateful aunt to snub her nieces and nephews on her birthday. But deep down, didn't they feel the malicious pleasure of someone who has just gained an afternoon? And free of guilt, after all, wasn't she the one who refused? Now, there she was, surrounded by people on all sides. And even lonelier than she would be locked in her room, where her objects reassured her memory which was growing insecure: baubles, photos. A desire to go quickly back, but, no, she had gone out for a special reason. I can't stay with you because I promised to meet my friends. My friends. Eleonora, with a broken pelvic bone, poor thing. Mariana, shuffling cards at some table, she hardly had the head to play blackjack anymore and had decided to learn bridge, wasn't it in style? Beatriz, shepherding her band of grandchildren while her daughter-in-law waddled about in her eighth month. And Elza was dead.

At the end of the block, a smaller cinema exhibited placards with scenes of hunters on safari. She looked with interest at the photo of a blond girl being attacked by a crocodile while the hunter (what a handsome man!) was pierced by a javelin. So far so good. The porter informed her that the film had already started some time ago, wouldn't she perhaps prefer to wait for the next showing? She thanked him but said she couldn't wait, it was getting colder, soon it would be sprinkling, winter, and she'd forgotten her umbrella. I forgot mine, too, he said, and she gave him a long look, wasn't he polite? In the middle of the barbarian invasion, there were still left a few of the old inhabitants of the town, rare, yes, and completely conquered (the porter's clothes were faded almost colorless) but preserving the feeling of respect for one's fellowman. No, she didn't ask for love, only for respect. She went down the steps holding onto the bannister. And under his watchful glance, she could swear it followed her, be careful on the steps! Moved, she went into the cozy darkness of the theater. Few people. She rested her handbag in her lap, opened the collar button of her blouse, and put on her glasses. On the screen, a bearded man with disheveled hair peeked through the foliage at a blond girl who had gone to bathe nude in the lake.

She sank deeper into the chair while the blond emerged from the bottom in the direction of the man, my heavens, here too? She fixed her attention on the couple laced together in the row ahead. They were kissing with such fury that the smacking sound was even clearer than the noise of the bodies crushing the foliage on the screen. A little farther on, in the same row, another couple, which had just arrived, were already breathlessly groping for each other, his hand searching under her clothes—did he find?—He found. She could feel the ardent breath of the bodies, which moved back and forth so intensely that the whole row of rough seats began to shake with the same rhythm. She shrank into herself. Just like animals. It was better not to pay any attention, think about something else, what? The headlines, she had an excellent memory, at school she could repeat an entire page after reading it over two or three times. "The Northeast goes through a very dry period," but where was the man with the flashlight? Weren't there any of those men? They used to be so attentive, the glowworms lighting their lanterns in the faces of the inconvenient, won't he appear? If he would just shine the light. She gripped the chair hard, and the leather seemed sticky, semen? She put on her gloves and held her legs close together. Dear Editor: first and foremost, I want to introduce myself, a retired teacher, citizen of São Paulo. Virgin. She closed her eyes, virgin, truly virgin, one doesn't write such things, but isn't it an important datum? She unbuttoned the second button, had the blouse shrunk in the wash or was her neck thicker? She sat there relaxed, disarranged, but let me stay this way awhile, it's dark, nobody's paying me any attention, they don't even where it's light, who cares, who? And if by chance the right thing should be this itself? This enjoyment, this humid pleasure in bodies. In words. This frothy panting like the river of girls back there, she had tried to detain it with her hoarse voice, her frowns, but it overflowed its banks, flooding everything, beds, houses, streets . . . and if the normal thing should be the happy sex of that girl sighing there in the front—and wasn't it created just for that? Virgin, Dear Editor. What do I know of this desire that has been boiling since biblical times, everything being fruitful and multiplying, people, animals, plants. Mama was afraid of sex, I inherited her fear—wasn't it from her I got it? Those girls from the Movement—so unrestrained, so free, are they really that way or are they just pretending? No shame at all, they talk about everything. Do everything. My embarrassment when I complained to Mama,

and her embarrassment when she took me to the lady
doctor, only a woman could examine my private parts, she
would lower her voice when she said *private parts*. My
daughter has a slight secretion, she said and made an
unhappy face. I stiffened my legs when the gloved finger
touched me and remembered her telling my grandmother
that she fulfilled her duties as a wife without any pleasure
up to the bitter end. Up to the bitter end, Mama? The
source of her suffering was now the source from which
flowed a flux. I tried to relax in the dreadful position
(you're so stiff, girl, like you were made of iron, relax, I
won't hurt you) and looked at Mama. She was a lachry-
mose statue, faithfully holding my hand. There, you can
put on your panties, ordered the voice from between my
legs. Nothing serious, you have a white fungus, sometimes
virgins get it. White fungus. It dried up, Dear Editor, it
dried up too. Everything dries up, old age is dry, all the
water evaporated out of me, my skin dried, my nails dried,
my hair which crackles and breaks when I comb it. Sexual
organs without secretion. Dry. It's been so long since they
dried completely up, a sealed fountain. The only difference is that in the Northeast, the rains come back.

On the screen, the safari man went into the tent and lay
down under the mosquito netting, smoking very sadly
because his lover (wife of his friend) was leaving, it was
more of a story of betrayal. She had heard so many,
starting with Mariana, when she came sobbing to ask her
not to get mad, don't condemn me, don't fight with me,
Mimi, but I'm in love with Afonso! Afonso Who, Mariana? I only know one, your husband's friend. Isn't he your
husband's friend? And Mariana's eyes opening like two
faucets, an intimate friend. She was implacable, argued,
you're crazy, Mariana, stark raving mad, why didn't you
at least choose a man from elsewhere, a stranger? And she
drying her face, perplexed, but Mimi, don't you understand? One ends up falling in love with those in one's own
circle. Afonso is very similar to my husband, similar to
me, we have the same tastes, go to the same places, and
one day you look at each other and then it's too late. Too
late, she kept repeating, disoriented, shaking her head, her

hair still its natural brown, it was later she streaked it with grayish blond. Don't condemn me, she pleaded so hard. I condemned her, yes, and with such rigor. Wasn't it out of pure envy? This feeling of superiority I have. Scorn. Envy, my heavens? Did I envy her unquiet life, unpredictable, full of happenings, rich in passion—was it envy then? Look at your antics, I told her the other day, and she laughed and her eyes moistened as if she were still young, youth is moisture. The closed pores retaining the water of the sap-filled flesh, what fruit does it remind one of, peaches? that we bite into and the juice runs warmly out—*we*? That others bite into, what do I know of this fruit? She laced her hands together on her lap. In the darkness her gloves seemed so white, as if they had never touched anything. She quickly folded her arms against her body so as not to brush her elbow against the man who sat in the seat next to hers. Eat with your wings folded, Mama used to tell me. Live with your wings folded, she might as well have said. Yes, there's my love for God. But can so much discipline, so much exactitude, be called love? If I had at least entered a convent, burned myself out in vigils, fasts, lacerating hands and feet in piety—what proof have I given of my devotion? It is God's will, Mama used to say, and I would repeat, it is God's will. But was it really? What do I know of His will? Is my grade higher, teacher? Only if your notebook is in order, without tears or blotches, covered in green transparent butter paper. Butter with or without salt. What do I know about this river with its turns and bends? Doesn't it finally flow into the heart? And isn't the heart irrigated by love?

She opened her handbag, took out a handkerchief, and dried her eyes. Through the misted-over lenses of her glasses, she could tell that the film was coming to an end, and she fervently wished it would go on, she didn't want the light to come on now, wait, I'm so disarranged, my heavens, let me button up, and this hair, what's become of my hairpin? She quickly patted the lapels of her jacket, unfastened the camellia, and put it away in the bottom of her bag. A tear slid around the edge of her mouth, cleaned it, why did I get so emotional? Like a foolish old woman, wait. I was starting to say that our city, Dear Editor, that this poor city—what is it that's wrong with this poor city? I ended up talking about other people, about myself, wait, let's start again, yes, the letter. Dear Editor: first and foremost. First and foremost, Dear Editor. Dear Editor: Dear Editor:

AVON BARD DISTINGUISHED LATIN AMERICAN FICTION